KNOT OVER

BOOK 3

THE OMEGA DEN

MISS RENAE

Contents

Blurb

MY PACK IS FINALLY back together, but after everything we've endured, happiness seems impossible to grasp.

I'm hiding secrets from my pack, and the demands from the Breeder facility are ones we refuse to surrender to. Those who've wronged us will pay.

This is knot over.

How can we protect our pack, our home, and our city? I don't know the answer yet, but one thing is certain: with my pack by my side, revenge will be mine.

And I won't stop until we've taken back everything that's ours.

KNOT OVER is the third and final book in The Omega Den Trilogy. But Sterling City Omegaverse isn't over. More to come in this world.

Tropes: Heat emergency, Age gap, MMFM, Breeding, DVP, Knotting

Trigger warning and content: murder, blood, stabbing, revenge, active drug addiction with withdraws, grief and depression

Playlist

(In no particular order)

Valkyrae, Fuslie & Ylona Garcia - Echoes

Wiz Khalifa - See You Again ft. Charlie Puth

Lose Control – Teddy Swims

Benson Boone - Slow It Down

Livingston - Last Man Standing

Dedication

TO MY FERAL ALPHA queen, Marla—

Knot Over and *The Omega Den* series as a whole are dedicated to you, not just because you love these characters as much as I do, but because of all the late nights we spent dissecting Vaughn, Creed, and Hux's stories. Thank you for being more than just a listener—you engaged, encouraged, and inspired me to dig deeper and write with more passion. (I'm better because of you.)

There were so many moments when I wanted to give up, when I didn't know what the hell I was doing. When imposter syndrome struck hard, you were there, pushing me to keep going. You believed in me when I struggled to believe in myself, and because of you, I was able to finish my first true series. GAWWW, it makes me emotional, and for the first time ever, I'm seriously proud of a book I've published.

Your belief in me made all the difference, and for that, I will always be grateful.

The friendship we've built is beautiful, and it's all thanks to the Chaotic Alphacorn chat on Facebook (huge thanks to Brittany, who has a real gift for bringing people together—and to all the alphas, authors, and PAs in that chat).

Marla, I didn't expect us to get so close so fast. You demanded my friend-ship and pushed away any doubt in my mind that you wanted me in your life. I can't imagine my life without you now. You've been the rock I didn't know I needed, and I hope you know how much that means to me.

Never once have you made me feel like I talk too much about my books. You've never made me feel guilty for being who I am—chaotic, crazy, and all. You accept me, flaws and all, and that acceptance has been one of the greatest gifts I've ever received.

You're feral. You're real. You're an alpha queen in every sense of the word LOL. You've got a friend in me for life, and there's no getting rid of me now—you're stuck with me, *bitch*.

Love you to pieces, my Feral Alphacorn. You're more than just a friend; you're my family.

CHAPTER 1

Kaylani

E VERYWHERE I TURN, BEX'S presence lingers.

I catch her scent in the fresh summer breeze, a hint of citrus floating through the air as I sit at her funeral, watching two little girls play on the freshly cut grass. It's like she's still here, woven into every detail of my life. I hear her in the soft hum of our favorite song that played on the radio on the way over, the one we used to belt out during late-night drives.

The sunset bleeds vibrant shades of orange and red across the horizon—just like her hair, just like her fiery spirit that will forever be missed.

Our family and friends gather to celebrate her life and my foster mom is even here in support. The last time I saw her was before Bex went missing—eight long months ago. Back then, everything was different.

I was different.

Our eyes meet across the crowd, and for a moment, the world falls away. All the changes, the distance between us, fades as I see the love shining in aunt Eden's eyes. Her familiar smile reaches out to me, and in that instant all the pain and confusion melt away, leaving only the warmth of her love. The tears I've been fighting back thicken painfully in my throat.

When someone you love is ripped from your life, it doesn't just leave a void—it shatters everything, leaving fragments of yourself scattered in their wake. Grief is a strange companion. It shifts and changes as the days pass. Sometimes it's a suffocating blanket, all-consuming. And other times it's a whisper, a reminder that nothing will ever fill the space left behind. My pack keeps telling me that time will heal, but they don't understand. I don't need to heal; I need answers. Bex's death wasn't just a tragic accident. It's a mystery wrapped in shadows with too many questions left unanswered.

Why would a mother let this happen to her child? What about the other omegas? Are they destined for the same fate? And what the hell is my pack going to do about it?

Anger flares within me, a sharp, uncontrollable wave that makes my leg start to bounce. The sun beats down, sweat forming on my brow, but it does nothing to quench the fire burning inside. Each beat of my heart fuels my rage, hot and relentless, until I feel like I might burst. They've taken so much from me—my peace, my choices, my best friend—and for what? Their greed? Their twisted sense of control?

I clench my fists, nails biting into my palms, and it's the pain that grounds me. They think they've won. They think I'll just lie down and accept this. But they're wrong. Dead wrong.

I will make them pay. Every single one of them.

Whether it's today, tomorrow, or years from now, I'll see them brought to their knees. And if I can't? If it's truly hopeless, then I'll go down swinging. I'd rather burn this entire world to the ground than let them break me.

The thought pulses in my veins, dark and consuming. It gives me purpose, gives me something to hold on to in the midst of the chaos.

I won't stop until they regret everything they've done.

Hux senses my distress, his hand softly resting on my thigh in silent support. I glance up at him and force a smile, though it barely touches my eyes. When was the last time I smiled out of genuine happiness? I can't remember. I'm not okay. How could I be?

My best friend was murdered, and her own mother played a part in it—someone I trusted. And now, the same drug that killed Bex is coursing through my veins, a secret I've kept from everyone.

I've found out it's a heat stimulant, a drug designed to control your cycle and push back the natural order. I didn't know much about it at first, only that it was dangerously addictive, a shortcut omegas took when they couldn't bear to face their heat. But now I know all too well how it latches on, making you feel like you're in control when you're anything but.

Keep my heat at bay? Check. Maintain my instincts? Check.

But the worst part? I don't know what will happen when I stop taking it. If I let my heat come. Already, I can feel it simmering just beneath the surface, a burning sensation creeping through my veins. It already feels nothing like any heat I've experienced before, and the thought of what might happen terrifies me.

I'm not ready to deal with that. Not yet.

I'd need help, but how could I tell them? Hux, Creed, Vaughn—they'd look at me with disappointment I couldn't bear. Because I've been willingly taking it since Bex died. I've ignored my own instincts, blinded by my desperation. I've been hiding my pain from my pack, pretending I can deal with this on my own. But I see them lurking in the shadows, watching me while battling their own demons.

Especially Hux. I don't know what happened to him and Bex in that basement. I don't know how deep their connection ran. I should be thankful they had each other when it mattered most, but there's a sick, twisted part of me that feels jealous.

How sick is that? To be envious that in her final moments, she wasn't alone? That someone was there for her, cared for her, tried to protect her when I couldn't.

But it should have been me.

Now I'm sitting here, surrounded by my pack, and I've never felt more alone. Hux is on my left, his strong presence barely holding back the storm raging inside me. Vaughn is on my right, the man who has protected me, held me during countless sleepless nights. Creed sits on the other side of Vaughn, his back rigid, jaw clenched so tightly I can almost hear it. He blames himself for Bex's death. But is that fair? She was my friend and I should have done something sooner. She was missing for four months. Four fucking months, and I did nothing. So no, if anyone is to blame, it's me.

The crowd around us begins to stir, moving toward Bex's casket as it's lowered into the ground, and a sudden gust of wind carries the unmistakable scent of tobacco. My heart skips a beat and I freeze, my entire body going rigid. I know I should be focused on the somber moment, paying my respects as Bex is laid to rest. But I can't tear my mind away from the oppressive sense of dread I feel at that scent.

Adam.

Over the past two months it feels like I've been haunted. I've caught whiffs of him, glimpsed fleeting shadows, and even heard his voice echo in the silence. It's as if he's stalking me from the fringes of my reality. I'm not sure if it's the Heat, the trauma of losing Bex, or some twisted mix of both, but it's driving me to the brink of madness.

My breaths come in sharp, uneven gasps as I struggle to maintain my composure. Just as I'm on the edge of losing it, I hear the hushed whispers, a ripple of murmurs that draw my attention. Following the gazes of the other mourners, I spot Sabrina, clad in black and making her way toward us. The sight sends a shiver down my spine, amplifying my sense of paranoia and fear.

"What the fuck is she doing here?" Creed growls, his voice low and dangerous. Vaughn places a hand on his knee. "Don't make a scene, love."

Creed turns to Vaughn, violence and hate burning in his green eyes. "Don't cause a scene?" he hisses. "She isn't welcome here."

Hux stands. "I'll deal with her," he says, his fingertips brushing my cheek as he passes by.

Hux's touch is fleeting, a ghost of comfort that lingers on my skin as he strides toward Sabrina. My heart pounds in my chest, a rhythm that matches the thunderous rage pulsing through my veins.

I can't take my eyes off Sabrina as she approaches, her black dress flowing like a dark shadow across the grass. Her face is unreadable, a mask of calm that only fuels the fire inside me. What right does she have to be here? After everything she's done—everything she's taken from us—how dare she show her face at Bex's funeral.

"Breathe doll," Vaughn whispers beside me, his voice a gentle command that washes the scent of chocolate over me. His hand moves to encircle my waist, grounding me, and I desperately cling to his strength. But it's not enough to quell the storm raging inside me.

Hux stops in front of Sabrina, blocking her path. His broad shoulders are tense, his stance protective, and for a moment they stand there in silence, an unspoken battle of wills raging between them. I can't hear what Hux says to her, but I see the way her eyes narrow, the brief flash of something—anger? Regret?—before she schools her features back into that infuriating calm.

That same calm I saw when we worked together in Sterling Hospital. The same calm I saw when I told her Bex was dead and she knew she wasn't. A growl of anger bubbles up my chest.

"She has no place here," Creed snarls under his breath, his fists clenched so tightly his knuckles are white. I can feel the tension rolling off him in waves, his need to protect—to strike—nearly overwhelming. But Vaughn's hand on his shoulder keeps him grounded, at least for now.

She tries to step around Hux, but he stands firm, an unyielding wall that blocks her path. His body is a solid barrier, keeping her from getting any closer to us. To me.

Finally, Sabrina speaks, her voice carrying on the breeze—soft but sharp enough to cut through the heavy silence. "I'm not here to cause trouble," she says, though an edge in her tone betrays her insincerity. "I came to pay my respects."

"Your respects?" Creed scoffs, disdain dripping from his voice. "You've got some fucking nerve, Sabrina."

Hux glances back at me, his bright blue eyes locking with mine. "I can make her leave, kitten. Whatever you want."

My heart twists, torn between wanting her gone and craving answers. I want her to suffer as we are, but more than anything, I need to understand what happened.

"Let her speak," I finally whisper, the words barely escaping my lips, but carrying weight. Hux steps aside, allowing Sabrina to approach. Though he remains close, ready to act if needed.

Sabrina advances slowly, her eyes darting between me and the rest of my pack. When she stops in front of me, she hesitates, searching for the right words.

I'm done waiting though.

"What do you want?" I ask, my voice cold and detached, a shield against the emotions threatening to break free.

"Kaylani, I'm so sorry. You have every right to hate me, but—"

Her attempt at remorse only fuels the fire inside me. I sneer, disgust curling my lips into something feral, something savage.

"Sorry?" I hiss, venom seeping into the word. "You think an apology will fix this? After everything you've done?"

Her composure wavers, and I see this for what it is—a desperate attempt to salvage something from the ruins she created. My heart aches with the dual pain of Bex's loss and the bitter betrayal of the woman before me. This is the same woman who lied, who covered up the truth and let me believe Bex was dead when she knew otherwise. The same woman who stood by, calm and collected, while my world shattered.

If anyone was to blame for Rebecca's death, it was Sabrina.

Sabrina takes a shaky breath, her resolve hardening. "I didn't come here to ask for forgiveness, Kaylani. I came because you need to know the truth. All of it."

"The truth?" I echo, my voice as cold as ice. "The truth, from you? Why should I believe anything you say?"

She flinches but stands her ground. "Because your life depends on it."

The weight of her words hits me like a stone. I want to turn away, to never see her again, but something in her eyes—raw and desperate—keeps me rooted to the spot.

"What are you talking about?" I whisper.

Sabrina glances at Hux and the two exchange a look, one I can't quite decipher right now. There is something there though, something unspoken that passes between them. Brina's hands tremble as she reaches into the pocket of her dress. My pack tenses, ready to react. But all she produces is a small vial filled with little white pills.

The vial in Sabrina's trembling hand sends a jolt of recognition through me. The drug—the same one she gave me, the one that killed my best friend.

Heat.

Sabrina's voice is barely audible, breaking with emotion. "This is what they wanted from me," she says, her hand trembling as she holds out the vial filled with little white pills. "This is what they used on Rebecca, on all those omegas at the estate."

I stare at the vial, memories of Bex's overdose flashing through my mind. My throat tightens, but I shove the thoughts away. I can't deal with that right now.

"And who exactly are 'they'?" Vaughn's voice cuts through the tension, sharp and demanding. Sabrina's gaze flicks nervously between Vaughn and Creed, who is glaring at her with barely contained fury.

"The founding families," she says softly, eyes flicking back to me. "They all want control and won't stop until they gain sole power over the city. The Sterlings, the Bramwells... and the Hounds. Stacy Bramwell was the one who pushed hardest, until she died. And now, the Hounds have it."

My heart skips a beat as suspicion coils around my fear. "You're not making any sense, Brina. What power? What do they want with a heat stimulant?"

She steps closer, her voice dropping to a whisper. "The power to control the alphas. The power to bend them to their will by controlling omegas."

The weight of her words hits me like a punch to the gut. The alphas... controlled by manipulating omegas? By controlling our heats, they control who we breed with, who forms packs. Bex died because of this. Because the Hounds and the others wanted more power.

"You knew this all along," Hux growls, stepping forward and half-blocking Sabrina from my view, his protective instincts flaring. "You knew that Bex and all those omegas were part of some twisted experiment. You supplied the drugs to Michelle, Sabrina. You made your own daughter a pawn to control alphas. *Tell her*!"

Tears well in Sabrina's eyes, but she nods, her voice trembling. "It's true. And now the Hounds want to use a feral alpha to experiment on. Force him into a rut with an omega on Heat."

Feral alpha. The term sends a shiver down my spine as memories of Adam flood back—what he tried to do to me at the estate. It wasn't the Adam I knew. Maybe it was the half made bond that made him that way or who his mother was. I wasn't sure, but he was the definition of evil. A surge of nausea rises in my throat. Feral alphas are driven mad by their instincts, consumed by ruts they can't control. Nothing good could come of any of this.

Creed's voice breaks through the haze. "They want to use Adam." His green eyes meet mine, the guilt in them heavy as he acknowledges the role his brother plays in all of this.

Sabrina nods again, more certain this time. "Yes. And they can't use him if he's bonded."

Hux growls beside me, his anger palpable, vibrating in the air between us. His silence suddenly feels like betrayal. For two months since Bex's death, he knew about this twisted plan, and knew what Michelle and Stacy had done. But he kept it from me. His eyes meet mine, and in them, I see guilt and regret carved deep.

"They'll come for Kaylani," Sabrina adds quietly, her words crashing over me like a tidal wave.

The ground seems to shift beneath my feet. Not only do Michelle and Adam want me dead, but now Titus, the leader of the Hounds, wants me gone too.

Creed's low, feral growl fills the room, his fury rippling out like a physical force. His caramel scent sharpens, laced with rage. Vaughn tightens his grip on Creed's shoulder, but even my calm beta can't mask the fire burning in his onyx eyes.

"I won't let that happen," Hux snarls, his voice a dark promise. "Titus will have to go through all of us first."

Sabrina nods, her gaze steady on mine. "Let me help you."

"Why would I trust you? After everything you've done?" I demand, bitterness lacing my words. "And Hux. Why didn't you tell me? For two months, you've been home, and not once did you think I needed to know any of this?"

Hux's face flushes with a mix of hurt and shame. "I thought I could protect you," he admits, his voice low. "I didn't want to add to your pain. I thought—"

"No. You don't get to decide anything for me. You're not my alpha."

Adam is. My inner voice reminds me.

Hux visibly recoils at my words, his spicy scent suddenly overwhelming. My heart shatters at the pain in his eyes, but it's the truth. My alpha is feral and unpredictable. And now, I'm wanted dead by a gang leader, and everything is spiraling out of control.

"Kay, please," Sabrina's voice trembles with desperation. "Let me help you. Let me make it right."

I stare at her, torn between simmering anger and a deep-seated need for vengeance. There's only one thing left to do: kill Adam before Titus comes for me.

A gentle touch lands on the small of my back, and I'm enveloped in the familiar, comforting scent of peaches. It's Eden. Her presence drives the rage from my body, replacing it with overwhelming grief. A full, ugly sob rips through me as I turn into her arms, pulling her close.

"Eden," I cry into her shoulder, my voice trembling with raw emotion. It's been so long since I've seen my foster mom, and having her here now is exactly what I need. Her familiar presence is a beacon in this storm of grief.

"I'm here, Kay Kay," Eden whispers, her voice a soothing balm to my shattered soul. "Let it out, dear. It's okay to grieve."

Tears stream down my cheeks as I cling to her. The dam I've been holding back finally breaks. The weight of everything—the loss of my best friend, the betrayal of Sabrina, the guilt of my inaction, and Hux's silence—crashes down on me all at once. I sob uncontrollably, feeling every emotion with a piercing intensity.

"I miss her, auntie," I choke out between sobs. "I miss her so much."

"I know, dearie," Eden murmurs, holding me close. "I know."

Her gaze snaps to Hux, her voice sharp and accusatory. "What is wrong with you, Owen Huxley? You should be ashamed of yourself. The day my bonus-daughter lays her best friend to rest, and you're letting this happen... Disappointing."

Her eyes then turn to Sabrina, the disapproval even more intense. "And you, Sabrina, should be ashamed of yourself. You stand here, pleading for Kaylani's trust after everything that's happened? You're the one to blame for her grief in the first place. Your medical license should be revoked. Promising to help her? Ridiculous. Kay doesn't need your promises right now—she needs safety and protection. It's time she comes home with me."

"Come on, dearie," Eden continues, her tone softening as she hugs me tightly. I blindly let her lead me away, clinging to her as I did when I lost my mom. She was there for me then, too. She's always been there when I needed her most.

"Kitten," Hux's voice calls after me, but it's drowned out by the roar of emotions crashing inside me. I'm seething with anger, drowning in sorrow, and suffocating under the weight of guilt.

I push those thoughts to the back of my subconscious, unable to process any of my grief right now. A numbing void settles over me, and I surrender to it, letting it shield me from the chaos until I'm ready to face it again.

CHAPTER 2

Kaylani

NOT WANTING TO GO back to the den, I allow myself to be taken to the one place I've always felt safe. Aunt Eden's house looks just as I remember, frozen in time. The familiar wraparound porch and the old swing creak gently in the breeze, triggering memories of lazy summer afternoons spent lost in books.

I follow Eden into my childhood home. The TV blares with children's cartoons, but I barely register it. It's been far too long since I've set foot in this house.

"Auntie Kay?" A small, excited voice cuts through my thoughts and I turn to see Ren hurtling toward me. Her disheveled black hair bounces with each step, her ten-year-old face lit up with pure joy.

"There's my favorite niece!" I exclaim, dropping to one knee to catch her in a tight hug. She's grown taller since I last saw her, but her mischievous grin hasn't changed a bit. "I'm your only niece," she says.

"What happened to your hair, Rennie? Did you decide to wrestle a tornado today?"

She giggles, a sound that instantly brightens my mood. A true and genuine joy wraps around me. One that I haven't felt in a long time.

"No! I was playing with the twins, and they're terrible at hair braiding."

"Clearly," I tease, pretending to inspect her wild mane with a critical eye. "It looks like a bird tried to build a nest in there."

Ren swats at my arm, laughing. "Auntie Kay, you're so silly! But I missed you."

"I missed you more," I say, pulling her close again. "You know, you're getting too big for me to pick up. What am I going to do when you're taller than me?"

"You'll just have to try harder!" Ren declares, puffing out her chest like a little warrior. I can't help but smile at her confidence. She looks just like Serenity, my foster sister.

"Where's your mommy?" I ask, finally releasing her from the hug but keeping her hand in mine.

"She's in the kitchen making cookies," Ren replies with a sly grin. "If you're nice to me, I might save you one."

I raise an eyebrow at her, feigning seriousness. "Oh, I see how it is. Bribery already? You've been spending too much time with the twins."

Ren shrugs playfully, clearly proud of herself. "Maybe, but I learned from the best."

I laugh and ruffle her hair, then give her a gentle nudge toward the stairs where the other kids Aunt Eden fosters are playing. She darts off, her laughter mixing with the innocent joy of the other children as they disappear from view.

Left standing in the doorway, I take a moment to soak in the surroundings. The familiar creak of the floorboards, the gentle hum of the old refrigerator, and the soft glow of sunlight filtering through the lace curtains—all of it feels like a balm to my weary soul. The familiar staircase I used to race Serenity up and down, the photos lining the walls, capturing moments of laughter and love, all serve as comforting reminders of simpler times.

I step further into the living room, letting my fingers graze the well-worn furniture and the framed photos that tell the story of our lives. Each picture is a snapshot of happiness, a memory frozen in time. I pause at one photo, it shows younger versions of Serenity and me, arms wrapped around each other, faces smeared with chocolate from one of Aunt Eden's baking sessions. The weight on my chest lightens, just a bit, as I allow the nostalgia to wash over me.

As I make my way toward the kitchen, a sense of calm settles over me, like being curled up in a nest on a cold winter's night in a warm blanket.

The sounds of familiar voices drift toward me, their light-hearted chatter a soothing contrast to the chaos of the past months. I force a smile onto my face as I push open the kitchen door, hoping to blend in with the normalcy that my childhood home always offers me.

Inside, Serenity and her alpha, Lorenzo Avelino, are seated at the table, chatting over mugs of coffee. Serenity's face lights up with surprise and delight as she spots me in the doorway, but that joy quickly turns to horror as she takes in my tear-streaked face and disheveled appearance.

I cringe as she rushes to me. I know I look horrible. I've been crying, and my makeup is probably ruined.

"Kay! Oh, sis, it's been too long," Serenity exclaims, quickly setting down her coffee and rushing over to wrap me in a tight hug. Her vanilla scent is comforting and familiar. Her arms around me are like a lifeline, and I cling to her, but the tears I thought I had under control spill over again. I catch Lorenzo's concerned gaze over her shoulder, and the fierce protectiveness in his eyes almost makes me break down completely.

"Who made you cry?" Lorenzo growls, his deep voice vibrating with barely contained anger. Before I can answer, he steps up and engulfs me in a big bear hug, lifting me off my feet and spinning me around in a playful circle. I squeal in surprise, as I half-heartedly slap his broad shoulder.

"Put me down, you big lug!" I protest, trying to sound indignant but failing miserably. His antics bring a genuine smile to my face for the first time in what feels like forever. Being home is exactly what I need right now.

But beneath my smile, a storm is brewing. I can't shake the anger that's been simmering since Bex's funeral—the raw edge of grief mingling with the bitter taste of betrayal. Hux knew about the twisted plans involving Michelle and Stacy. Maybe he didn't know exactly what the Hounds were planning. But still, how could he keep something like that from me? It feels like a betrayal of the bond we share, which is supposed to mean everything. Instead, it's overshadowed by him keeping secrets. Not to mention the threat of Adam, the mate I need to break free from before I can truly be a part of Hux's pack.

By either his death or mine...

Creed, Vaughn, and Hux are all I truly want. I want what Serenity, Lorenzo, and Dario have. A family of my own.

I'm trapped in this painful limbo.

Lorenzo finally puts me down, holding me out to look at me. "There. That's better," he says, referring to the grin on my face. If only he knew how fragile that smile truly is, how it's barely holding together the pieces of my broken heart.

"Where's Dario?" I ask, looking around for the third member of their pack, who's always been like a big brother to me.

"He's out getting groceries," Lorenzo replies warmly. "He'll be back soon. It's so good to see you, Kaylani. You have no idea how much little Rennie missed you."

My sister's smile widens, her hand instinctively resting on her stomach—a gesture I don't miss. "I sent Dario out on a special mission. I've been having these wild cravings lately."

Lorenzo chuckles, shaking his head. "Wild cravings is putting it mildly. We're talking pickles and ice cream at three in the morning."

I laugh, the sound feeling foreign but a welcome reprieve. "Pregnancy cravings? You're...?" My eyes widen with realization and excitement.

Serenity's smile grows even wider as she nods. "Yep! We're expecting our second child. I've been meaning to tell you, but with everything going on, it slipped through the cracks."

A rush of joy and relief floods through me, momentarily lifting the heavy weight of grief. "Oh my god, Serenity! That's amazing news!" I reach out and hug her tightly, careful of her growing belly. "Congratulations! I'm so happy for your pack."

She hugs me back, her happiness radiating. "Thank you, Kay. We're thrilled. Ren is excited to be a big sister."

Lorenzo's eyes shine with pride as he adds, "It's a blessing, Kay. Rennie is almost ten now and we've been wanting to expand our pack for a while."

I nod, trying to hold onto the joy of this moment, but it slips through my fingers like sand. I'm happy for Serenity, I truly am, but the reminder of what she has—what I might never have—cuts deep.

Hux and I could have had this, a family, a future, but Adam's bond chains me to the past, to a man who doesn't even care. And now I don't even know if I can trust Hux.

I can't help but wonder if things would be different if he'd just been honest with me. If he'd trusted me enough to tell me the truth, maybe I wouldn't feel so lost, so betrayed.

"It's good to have you home," Serenity says softly, sensing my shift in mood.

"Yeah," I agree, squeezing her hand. "It's good to be home. Sometimes you just need your family."

Aunt Eden, who's been quietly watching from the doorway, smiles warmly. "This will always be your home, dearie. Let me cook something for you. You look like you could use a good meal," she says, her voice filled with motherly concern.

Eden has always made us food when we're down. Whether it was because of a bad grade or a boyfriend breaking up with me, she would whip up my favorite pancakes and listen to me cry. Aunt Eden believes in the healing power of her cooking, and those pancakes, cooked in bacon grease, are legendary—a comfort that soothes anyone who tastes them. As she moves around the kitchen, I feel a sense of relief wash over me, knowing that I'm in good hands here, surrounded by family.

Tears threaten to spill from my eyes as I sink into a chair, overwhelmed by the flood of emotions and memories that being here brings. This kitchen has witnessed countless moments of joy and sorrow, and in this moment, it offers me the refuge I desperately crave.

"Thanks, Auntie. I've missed home so much," I reply, my voice soft with emotion. "Everything's been so... chaotic lately," I admit, my gaze drifting toward the window, where sunlight dances on the leaves outside. "With Bex's death and all."

Those two words—Bex's death—never get easier to say. Talking to my family about my best friend being gone feels like a dam breaking, releasing all the emotions I've held back. Out of everything that's happened in the last several months, this is the one thing I'll never get over.

Serenity places a hand on my shoulder, her eyes filled with empathy. "I'm so sorry about Rebecca. I wanted to go to her funeral, but I had to stay with Ren."

I take a deep breath, collecting myself. Serenity was always like a sister to me. Though she's a bit older and we had different sets of friends, she's always treated me like family. That's just how the Jacobs are.

Eden adopted her niece and nephew when they were very young, and ever since, the Jacobs household has been a refuge for strays like me. "Where is Shade?" I ask.

"He will be down soon." Aunt Eden says as she bustles around the kitchen, the clinking of dishes and the sizzle of bacon providing a comforting backdrop to our conversation. The aroma of pancakes soon fills the air, bringing with it a sense of nostalgia and warmth.

Shade walks into the kitchen, heading straight to Aunt Eden and giving her a kiss on the cheek. "Morning, Auntie," he murmurs before turning to face me and Serenity. I can practically feel the tension radiating off Shade. His mossy eyes settle on me, narrowing with suspicion.

"What the fuck happened to you, Kay Kay?" he growls, using my child-hood nickname, stomping across the room to take my face in his massive callused hands.

I frown at his touch and pull my chin free. "Nothing," I say, my voice barely above a whisper.

"It doesn't look like nothing. Who made you cry?" Shade growls again, his tone laced with an alpha-bark.

"Shade Jacobs!" Aunt Eden exclaims, her voice firm. "You leave that poor girl alone right now. She's been through enough and needs to eat and rest. Not worry about some alpha barking commands at her! Not in my house, young man."

Shade cringes at Aunt Eden's outburst, realizing he's overstepped. Serenity and I exchange a glance and she snorts, covering her mouth to stifle a laugh. I chuckle along with her. It's like old times all over again—Shade being the overprotective brother, demanding we tell him everything, and Auntie reprimanding him with her motherly authority. The familiar dynamic brings a sense of comfort.

"Some things never change," I say, mock-whispering as I try to hold back another peal of laughter.

Serenity lets out a giggle, her eyes sparkling with mischief. "She's right, Shade. You're as predictable as ever," she teases, nudging him playfully.

Shade's expression softens, and I can see a hint of amusement breaking through his serious demeanor. "Very funny. A regular comedian," he mutters, though the corner of his lips betrays a twitch of a smile. "Now, let's eat before Auntie starts scolding us for not appreciating her cooking."

Aunt Eden chuckles from where she's bustling around the kitchen. "I heard that, young man," she calls out playfully, causing us all to laugh.

Shade is a massive alpha, broad and thick as a tree. Despite being the youngest of us three, he always seemed older than his years. He reminds me, for a moment, of Vaughn, and a pang of guilt circles through me. I had left the service so abruptly, and he and Creed are likely worried sick about me. If I had my phone, I would have texted them already, but in my rush to leave I had forgotten it in Hux's car.

"Tell me something, okay?" Shade's voice is soft, but his eyes are intense, searching mine. "I'm going crazy here."

I nod, knowing I have to relive the painful events for my family's sake. The plate of pancakes in front of me, with Aunt Eden's cheerful smiley face made of whipped cream and chocolate chips, stares back at me as I take a moment. I take a deep breath, trying to steady my voice as I begin.

"Adam went feral when I didn't complete the bond with him," I start, my voice trembling. "The Hounds, Michelle. They want that bond broken. By any means necessary." My chest tightens as I speak, and I see the rage in Shade's eyes growing. He remains silent but seethes with barely contained fury.

"I had to come home," I murmur with a shrug, pushing the whipped cream around with my fork. "To the one place I've always felt safe."

Shade's jaw tightens further, his fists clenched so hard his knuckles turn white. The air between us crackles with his barely restrained anger. As I finish speaking, he reaches across the table, placing his large hand gently on mine.

"Kay Kay, you don't have to bear this alone. We're family. We'll face this together," he says, his voice deep and filled with reassurance.

I look up at him, my eyes welling with tears. "Thanks, Shade. It means more than you know."

Lorenzo, who's been quietly observing, finally chimes in. "As an alpha, we don't always get it right, Kay. We make mistakes too. But it sounds like Hux is a good alpha at heart, and he deserves a chance to explain himself," he says thoughtfully. His gaze shifts to Serenity, his eyes softening with adoration, and he gives her a playful wink.

Serenity's lips curl into a knowing smile as she nods. "Yep, sometimes they think they have all the answers. We just have to remind them that we omegas are strong too," she teases, her voice light and affectionate. She turns her attention back to me, her expression serious yet supportive. "Stick with your pack, sis. Don't run away from them."

I manage a weak smile, feeling a flicker of hope despite the heaviness of the situation. "Maybe you're right," I say softly, letting their support sink in.

As we sit together, the aroma of pancakes and the gentle clinking of dishes provide a comforting backdrop. The familiar, loving atmosphere of Aunt Eden's kitchen starts to ease some of the tension in my shoulders.

It's good to be home.

CHAPTER 3

Hux

I PACE BACK AND forth in my living room as Candi sits on the couch, half-heartedly watching a news broadcast. The light from the screen flickers across the room, casting long shadows that only seem to heighten my unease. Creed and Vaughn are still asleep, but I tossed and turned all night and couldn't take it anymore. I've gotten used to Kay sleeping beside me, her warmth anchoring me through the night. Now, without her, it feels like a piece of me is missing, and the bed feels too damn big.

I'm caught between the instinctual need to track her down and bring her back where she belongs, and the logical part of me that understands she needs space. She's hurt because I didn't tell her everything about what happened to me and Rebecca in that basement, and the full extent of Michelle's twisted plans. I know Michelle wants Kay dead and Candice in her place, but since the estate raid, she hasn't made a move to achieve that.

I thought we were safe.

I'm struggling with the guilt that I failed Rebecca, that I couldn't protect my kitten's best friend, and that I'm failing to protect my sister and my pack. My mind reels with the weight of it all, Michelle's dark confession in that basement, her intention to break Adam's bond and force Candice into a fate she doesn't want. It's all too much. I thought the Hounds' betrayal and their theft of all those omegas had ruined Michelle's plans.

Yes, I should have shared the truth with my pack, but I thought I was protecting them. I tug at my beard in frustration, my thoughts a tangled mess. I was so consumed with guilt that I failed to see the bigger picture.

I believed Stacy's death had stopped Jordan's plans. I thought we'd dodged a bullet when Titus shot her, convinced it had blocked Jordan's path to the alpha position of the next generation pack. This should have meant Creed was safe from being forced into a bond he didn't want.

But now, I'm starting to see that it was never just about Jordan or Creed or Candice. It was about gaining control over my city. The Hounds want to control all unmated omegas in Sterling, believing that using the Heat stimulant and forcing a feral alpha into a rut will give them that power.

And that feral alpha just happens to be the one who directly affects my family.

I should have told Kay what I knew. Maybe then when we found out the full extent of the Hounds plans it wouldn't have been so much of a shock.

She has every right to be furious with me.

The thought of her out there, away from the pack, away from me, makes my skin itch with the urge to hunt her down. The idea that she could slip away for good sends a cold wave of panic through me.

I've fought too hard to let that happen.

This gnawing anxiety is worse than anything I've ever felt. Not even the basement of the Sterling estate compares to this. The memory of those cold, concrete walls closing in on me, the suffocating darkness, and the relentless dread of what they'd do next is nothing compared to the hollow ache in my chest now. Back then, I knew I was fighting for my life, and that fear kept me sharp, kept me focused.

But this?

If she denied me as her alpha, I'm not sure I could bear it. Being trapped was a nightmare, but at least I knew where I stood. I knew my enemy. But this uncertainty, this not knowing where Kay is or if she'll come back—that's a different kind of torture. One that eats away at me from the inside, slowly unraveling every thread of control I've ever had.

And I can't stand it.

"Stop that," Candi snaps, leaning over the back of the leather couch to scowl at me. "Your pacing is driving me insane, Owen." I stop mid-step and glare at my sister. But she remains unfazed and just smirks at my discomfort, irritating me further.

"I'm making you insane? Please," I scoff, pointing a finger at her. "You don't need any help in that department."

Candi rolls her eyes dramatically, looking up at the ceiling like she's searching for patience. "Stop deflecting," she demands, patting the couch cushion. "Now. Sit, spill."

"What am I, a dog?" I snap.

Candi just smiles at me sweetly and I sigh, crossing the room toward her.

"You're so damn bossy," I growl, but do as she says, flopping down next to her. "And you say I'm driving you insane," I taunt with a grin.

There's something about my sister that brings out my inner child, and bickering with her is easier than talking about what's really bothering me.

"Please, Owen. You're the one who's pacing like a caged tiger at six a.m. It's giving me a headache," she whines, massaging her temples.

"You know I pace when I'm thinking, Candice." I pout, crossing my arms defensively.

She raises a pierced eyebrow. "Thinking, huh? That's new for you."

"Well, someone's gotta do it around here. Can't have you hogging the shared brain cell." I grin, unable to resist teasing her back.

"Shut up. We know who's had our brain cell this whole time. Spoiler alert," she whispers. "It isn't you."

"Well, maybe all my problems are your fault then," I counter. "Since you don't know how to share."

She snorts, tossing a pillow in my direction. I catch it and tuck it under my arm.

Candi shakes her head. "Nah, if that were true you'd be a lot more interesting."

I roll my eyes, but there's a smile tugging at the corners of my lips. "Right, because my life is just so dull."

She nudges my shoulder playfully. "You know what I mean, Owen. You're the responsible one, the steady rock we all lean on."

"Yeah, and you're the wild card," I retort, teasingly.

Candi grins. "Someone's gotta keep things interesting."

I glance at her, the warmth of our banter easing some of the tension coiled in my chest. It reminds me why I love having my sister around.

"I missed you," I admit, my tone getting more serious.

Candi's expression softens, her eyes meeting mine. "I missed you too, big bro."

I give her a half-smile, feeling a lump form in my throat. "You know, for a pain in the ass, you're not so bad."

She nudges me again, a playful glint in her eyes. "Now stop deflecting and tell me what's got you running laps this morning."

I gaze at my closed bedroom door. "You want to know what got me through these last few months?" Emotion lodges in my throat like a golf ball. "It's Kaylani..." I glance at my sister. "I promised you I'd never bond a pack. That I wouldn't leave you unprotected."

She sighs, "That was when I was fifteen, Owen. I'm twenty-two now. I don't need you to protect me anymore."

I study her, admiring the strength that's always defined Candi. She's tough, fierce, and independent—a force to be reckoned with. But beneath that exterior, there's a vulnerability I know too well. It's what's kept me tethered to her, what made me vow to protect her at all costs. Candi is all I have left and not telling her Michelle's plans for her sooner was a gnawing guilt that ate away at my insides.

"I love her, Candice," I confess, my voice barely above a whisper. "I have since I met her here at the club."

Candi's piercing blue eyes soften with understanding. "Have you told her how you feel?" she asks gently.

I shake my head, the knot in my stomach tightening. The fear of rejection paralyzes me.

"Just be an alpha. Tell Kaylani how you feel."

"What if she rejects me?" I voice my insecurities.

"Seriously, Owen?" Candi retorts, frustration creeping into her tone. "That girl has slept in your bed waiting for you to come home for months. Alpha-up and tell her how you feel."

I sigh heavily. Maybe she's right.

"Speaking of sharing feelings," she starts, her voice shifting, "there's something I need to talk to you about too."

I meet her gaze, noting the determination etched in her expression. "What's on your mind?"

She takes a deep breath, her resolve clear. "I've been thinking about the Omega Den," she begins, her voice firm. "About reopening it."

My heart clenches at the mention of the Den. The memories flood back—Bex being omega-napped from our back alley, Vaughn being stabbed, and the time I nearly killed an alpha, leading to my arrest. The fear of putting our family at risk again gnaws at me.

"Candi," I start, my tone cautious. "I don't know if that's a good idea. It's not safe."

Her eyes flash with defiance as she gets to her feet, pacing before turning back to face me. "I know the risks," she retorts. "But you, more than anyone, understand that the Den is more than just a club. It's a sanctuary for unmated omegas, a place where they can feel safe and supported during their heat. They deserve that, especially with everything the Sterlings and the Hounds are doing!"

She points at the muted TV, anger flaring in her voice. "You know Michelle is saying that the Hounds were keeping those omegas at her estate without her knowledge? That it's even more reason to have the Sanctuary open," she says with disgust. "A way to honor those that have been lost," she mocks Michelle's speech.

"It's bullshit. Plus, she's even naming it after Stacy. The Bramwell Sanctuary," she spits. "It's nothing more than a breeder facility, and you know it."

Her words hit hard, the frustration and determination in her eyes mirroring my own. The Den was our safe haven, a place we built together for omegas who had nowhere else to turn. But reopening it means stepping back into the line of fire, facing the dangers that nearly tore us apart once before.

Yet, deep down, I know Candi's right. The world hasn't changed, and those omegas still need a sanctuary. If we don't fight for them, who will?

I run a hand through my hair, torn between my instinct to protect my family and my sister's fervent belief in the Omega Den's importance. At one point in time, I would have agreed with her. But now? With three omegas living under my roof? The stakes feel higher.

"I understand where you're coming from—" I start.

"—But?" Candi interjects, hands on her hips, already sensing the resistance in my voice.

"But we can't ignore the dangers that have happened in our club either. We can't risk it." I shake my head, feeling the weight of responsibility press down on me as I stand to face her.

Candi lifts her gaze to mine, eyes narrowing with determination. "We can't let fear dictate our decisions. We have to fight for what we believe in, for the safety and well-being of our city."

"I understand what you're saying, but you know what happened the last time the Den was open. It's not just about the omegas' safety. It's about our family's safety too." My voice softens, hoping she understands the depth of my concern.

She meets my gaze, her eyes sharp. "But we have to do something. We can't just sit back and let the Sterlings and the Hounds dictate our lives."

Her words hit me like a punch to the gut. As much as I hate to admit it, she's right. We can't let fear control us. We have to fight for what we believe in—for what the Omega Den has always stood for: hope.

Damn it.

"Alright," I relent, my voice heavy with resignation. "But you're the one with the brain cell, remember? How do you suggest we maintain the Den?"

Candi's eyes harden with resolve. "Vaughn," she says simply.

My brows furrow in skepticism. "My beta can't be the only form of security the club has," I counter, knowing we need more than just Vaughn's strength to keep everyone safe.

She smirks, clearly pleased with herself, like I've just walked right into her grand plan. "*Your* beta?" she teases, and I groan inwardly. She's just maneuvered me into admitting my claim over my pack.

"Yes, my beta," I growl, irritation lacing my words as Candi chuckles triumphantly. "Shut up," I grumble, not in the mood for her playful ribbing.

"Vaughn has the Steel Serpents backing him, does he not?" she continues, crossing her arms over her chest and raising a brow in challenge.

I sigh, realizing the logic in her words. "I'll try to talk to the MC. Maybe Vaughn can arrange a meeting," I relent. "But first, let's get Kay safely home. She doesn't need more stress right now."

A smile spreads across Candi's face, the kind that says she's not done with me yet. "Yep, and you need to convince your pack that all of us need to be living under the same roof."

FUCK.

My sister's right again, and it's a realization that hits hard. Bringing the pack together under one roof means facing not only the physical challenges but the emotional ones as well. Kaylani, Creed, Vaughn—hell, even Candi—all of them are relying on me, and now this plan to reopen the Den is only going to add to that burden.

But as much as I want to fight it, I know Candi's right. It's time to bring our pack together, to face the future with a united front, no matter the risks.

"Fine," I mutter, the word tasting like defeat on my tongue. "But we're doing this my way."

Candi grins, knowing she's won this round. "Wouldn't have it any other way, big brother."

As much as her confidence irritates me, it's also the only thing keeping me grounded right now. We're in this together, for better or worse, and I just have to hope we're making the right choices.

CHAPTER 4
Kaylani

COMING DOWN THE STAIRS, I head straight to the kitchen, the aroma of freshly brewed coffee already calling to me. As I reach the threshold, I pause, surprised to see Sheriff Liam Bradshaw sitting at the breakfast nook, nursing a cup of coffee while Aunt Eden fusses over him.

"You haven't been here in months, Liam. You work too much," she reprimands him, her tone half-motherly, half-annoyed.

Liam gives her a sheepish grin, running a hand through his tousled hair. "I missed you too, Ms. Jacobs," he teases, his voice warm and familiar.

"Liam, how many times do I have to tell you? It's Eden."

Liam shrugs, chuckling, but the humor fades when he notices me standing in the doorway. His eyes meet mine, and I can see the concern etched in his features. It's strange seeing him in casual jeans and a button-up shirt. There's no sheriff's badge or uniform in sight, and my tense shoulders relax slightly. I don't need an interrogation this early in the morning, especially not from Shade's best friend.

"Hey, Kaylani," Liam greets, his voice a mix of worry and familiarity.

"Morning," I grumble, heading straight toward the coffee pot. I don't have the energy for Liam's questioning right now.

I have a date with a porch swing.

I pour myself a mug of coffee, savoring the rich aroma as it fills the room. The weight of the last few days feels a little lighter with the familiar routine. As I turn to head out to the porch, Liam's voice stops me.

"Kay, can we talk for a minute?"

I pause, glancing back at Liam. His expression is serious, and I know this isn't just a casual visit. With a sigh, I nod and take a seat across from him at the breakfast nook. Aunt Eden pats my shoulder gently before stepping out to give us some privacy.

"Depends on what about," I say, trying to keep my tone light despite the sinking feeling in my stomach.

Liam leans forward, his concern deepening. "The coroner said Bex died from an overdose? Where was she all these months? What really happened to her, Kay?"

His questions come fast, one after another, his voice tinged with frustration. I swallow hard, the memory of Bex's overdose still raw. "It's complicated, Liam," I say, my voice barely above a whisper.

Liam nods, his eyes never leaving mine. "Let me put away whoever is responsible," he murmurs.

I scoff. "If only it were that simple. I told you what Adam did to me, Liam. On the record," I snap. "And still, he walks free. The Hounds blew up the estate, and I don't see you arresting any of them for their involvement." My gaze hardens as I take in the man sitting across from me. "What exactly can you do? Your partner, Shari Ledger, is on the Sterling payroll and we both know it. Her brother Dane was the alpha Hux *'murdered,'*" I say, using my fingers to make air quotes. "Hux didn't actually kill him, Liam. And now Shari's tangled up in Michelle's web too. So what can you do, Liam, really?"

Liam's jaw tightens, frustration evident in his eyes, but I shake my head, averting my gaze. My hands tremble slightly as I wrap them around my mug and take a sip, hoping the warmth will steady me.

"I know it seems like nothing is being done, but we're working on it. Adam's case is complicated—his connections make it tough to bring him down. And the Hounds... they're slippery. But I'm not giving up, Kay. I promise you that."

I let out a bitter laugh. "Promises don't mean much when people like Titus and Michelle are still out there ruining lives and kidnapping omegas."

He leans closer, his voice low and intense. "I care about you, Kay. More than you know. You're Shade's sister, and I won't stop until those who hurt you and Bex are brought to justice. But bringing down Michelle or Titus won't be easy."

I shiver at the mention of my ex, but I see the logic in Liam's words. Removing Adam weakens their power, and that's a crucial first step. Plus, with Adam gone, maybe I can finally start to move on.

"Go on," I encourage, giving him my full attention.

"I need your help. Tell me everything you know about the Hounds' operations. The more we know, the better our chances."

I hesitate, the weight of what I'm about to share heavy on my shoulders. "You really think you can make a difference?"

"Yes, but I can't do it alone. We need to be smart about this."

I take a deep breath, considering his words. Bex deserves justice, and I could have a chance at happiness with Hux, Creed, and Vaughn. No, Michelle's twisted plan to open the sanctuary wouldn't be stopped. Yet. But it would be a start.

"Alright," I say finally. "I'll tell you everything. But you have to promise me you'll be careful. Michelle doesn't just hurt people—she destroys them. And if you think for one second Michelle isn't behind everything that happens in Sterling City—"

Liam raises a hand to stop my rant. "Kay, I know how dangerous she is. That's why we need a solid plan and evidence. We have to find her weak spots and take out her pawns before we go after the queen."

I nod. "Michelle's got eyes everywhere. She's got cops on her payroll, like Shari Ledger, and leverage over half the town."

Liam's expression darkens at the mention of Shari, but he doesn't comment. "And the stimulant that killed Bex?"

My stomach sinks at the thought of Sabrina's betrayal. "Sabrina was sup-
plying them," I admit, my voice wavering. "Jordan, Titus's son, gave Bex
more than she could handle. I think he was sending a message during the
raid. But I'm not sure."

But Jordan's motives and Sabrina's betrayal weren't the focus right now.
What mattered was making sure we hit back at the Hounds just as hard.
We need to take out a key player in their game and our best bet is Adam. A
part of me wishes I had let Vaughn kill Adam that night he tried to rape me.
But if Michelle was willing to fabricate charges against Hux, what would
she do to someone she considered a stray?

I shook my head, pushing away the regret. My pack wouldn't be involved
in this. I wouldn't let anyone else I cared about get hurt by Adam Sterling.
This was my responsibility. I was the one who was bitten by an alpha and
didn't return the bite. He went feral because of the half-completed bond,
and now it's up to me to stop him once and for all.

I look back up at Liam Bradshaw, the authority I know I can trust. The
justice system might be corrupt, but he isn't. He's a good alpha, and I trust
that he will help me see this through. He might not like my plan, but it
doesn't matter.

Liam's jaw tightens as he sees the determination in my eyes. "Adam needs
to pay for what he did to you, Kay," he growls. "I'll help you take him down.
I promise you that."

I look at him, searching for doubt and finding none. "Alright. But if we're
doing this, we do it my way. Michelle won't hesitate to hurt anyone who
stands in her way. We have to be prepared for anything. Especially if we
plan to take down her son. She won't let him go down without a fight."

"We will be," Liam assures me, his eyes burning with determination. "We'll take Adam down together. Hit Michelle and Titus with the loss of their prized alpha."

I take a deep breath, feeling a mix of fear and resolve. "We need to gather more intel first. Why do Michelle and the Hounds need these omegas to be on Heat? What does Adam, or any feral alpha, have to do with it? We need to understand the full scope."

Liam leans forward, eyes fixed on mine. "Do you have any idea where we can start?"

"Liam," I hesitate, my voice barely above a whisper, "this isn't just about taking down Adam or Michelle. It's about dismantling a network that's been built over years, woven into Sterling City's fabric."

Liam's gaze is unwavering. "I know, Kay. And I'm ready to do whatever it takes. But I need you to trust me. We can't let fear paralyze us. We need to act, and we need to be smart about it."

I take a deep breath, my heart pounding. Trust is a luxury, but Liam's determination is infectious. Despite my doubts, I nod.

"They're using the omegas as leverage, Liam," I say, voice steady despite my turmoil. "The Heat drug, the Bramwell Sanctuary. It's all about control. Adam's more than just Michelle's son. He's a symbol of their power. If we can take him down, it will significantly disrupt their empire."

Liam's jaw tightens, fists clenched on the table. "Then we'll hit them where it hurts the most. But we need allies, people we can trust. We need more than just rumors. We need solid evidence."

I nod, fear and anger mixing inside me. "I'll get you what you need. But we do it my way. No rushing in, no half-baked plans. We can't afford mistakes."

"Agreed," Liam says firmly. "We'll be methodical and precise. We'll dismantle their operation piece by piece."

A heavy silence settles between us, the enormity of our plan hanging like a storm cloud. But beneath the fear and anger, a flicker of hope persists.

"For Bex," I whisper, a vow and plea. "And for every omega, they've hurt."

Liam reaches across the table, his hand covering mine. "For Bex," he echoes, determination mirroring mine. "And for you, Kay. We'll make sure Adam never hurts anyone again."

CHAPTER 5

Creed

T HE RUMBLE OF MOTORCYCLE engines vibrates through the street, sending a jolt of adrenaline through my veins. My heart pounds against my ribs like a war drum. Each beat is a reminder of the stakes.

I run a nervous hand through my overgrown hair, the messy strands brushing against my fingers. *Shit*, I really need a haircut. My reflection in the bar's mirror is a testament to my anxiety—disheveled and out of sync with the calm facade I'm desperately trying to maintain.

I let out a sharp breath, trying to calm myself, but nothing is helping. Inhale. Exhale. I try to steady the storm of anxiety brewing inside me, but it feels like a hurricane. I've only met a few members of the Serpents so far—mainly Ghost.

And let's just say the first impression I made was less than stellar.

Showing up at the MC's compound, drunk and belligerent, wasn't exactly the best way to make a good impression. The memory makes me cringe, a hot flush of shame creeping up my neck. This is Vaughn's family, and I desperately need this to go well.

My omega instincts are practically screaming for Viper's approval.

But with my mother's reputation, I can't shake the nagging fear that he might already have his mind made up about me. The thought of them blaming me for the ongoing rivalry sends my nerves into overdrive, each second feeling like a ticking bomb. My hands tremble slightly as I wipe them on my shirt, trying to ignore the growing sense of dread.

"Stop looking like someone kicked your puppy, Creed," Candi drawls. "We need the MC and any of the Hounds not under Michelle's thumb on our side, and we have to convince the Serpents to help us today, we can't wait any longer. Plus, we need to bring Kay home. It's not about you and Vaughn's relationship right now, okay?"

My gaze flickers to her, my stomach knotting with unease. I force a tight-lipped smile. I know she's right. There's more at stake than my personal insecurities, and I've missed Kaylani terribly these past few days.

I really need tiny to come home.

Her absence has only amplified the tension among our pack, especially with Hux keeping things from us. I trust my alpha, but the secrecy has left a bitter taste in my mouth. Vaughn and I should have been brought into the loop.

"Easier said than done. Viper's not exactly known for being reasonable. He's a biker Candi."

She rolls her eyes, leaning closer as her voice softens, losing some of its edge. "Look, I know you're worried about Vaughn's family approving of you, but this isn't just about you two. It's bigger than that. We're talking about the Den, about protecting what we've built here. You've got to keep your head in the game."

I nod, swallowing hard. Her words resonate, but the gnawing fear doesn't dissipate easily. "Yeah, you're right. It's just... what if they see me as a liability? Vaughn's already taking a risk being with me, and if they decide I'm more trouble than I'm worth—"

"Stop," Candi interrupts, her tone firm, almost like a shield against my spiraling thoughts. "You're not a liability, Creed. You're strong, and you've got more fight in you than anyone gives you credit for. You're nothing like your family. Vaughn sees that, and so will they. But you have to show them. Don't let your fear get in the way."

I take a deep breath, letting her confidence wash over me like a calming wave. "Thanks, Candi. I needed that."

She smiles, a genuine warmth in her eyes that momentarily chases away the shadows. "That's what I'm here for. Now, get your ass together and let's show these alphas what we're made of. And remember. If life gives you lemons..."

I manage a small grin, the tension easing just a bit as her support bolsters my resolve. "Punch it in the face and demand chocolate."

Candi's laughter rings out. "Yes, exactly that."

The roar of motorcycles momentarily drowns the sound out as they pull up in the parking lot. My nerves tingle with heightened anticipation as I turn to watch three bikes come to a halt. The central rider dismounts first, pulling off his helmet to reveal an older man with tattoos crawling up his neck and shoulders, disappearing beneath his cut. He looks to be in his forties, around the same age as Hux.

This must be Viper.

The resemblance between Vaughn and his uncle is striking—they share the same muscular build and imposing presence. The other two riders follow suit, one clad in sunglasses and a beanie that obscures most of his face, and the other shorter and stockier, a contrast to Viper's tall and broad frame. As they approach the entrance, the guy with the sunglasses opens the door first. I recognize him as Ghost. He scans the room with a practiced eye before stationing himself by the entrance.

Well, at least I don't have to talk to Ghost right now.

"You must be Creed. The omega my nephew left my club for," Viper's deep voice rumbles, pulling me from my thoughts. I suppress a cringe as I cross the room, trying to keep my movements steady despite the clenching tension in my stomach.

Extending a sweaty palm, I offer it to him. For a moment, Viper's dark eyes rake over me, assessing. I swallow thickly, feeling exposed under his scrutiny. His gaze is intense, like a predator assessing its prey. And his alpha scent is potent and dominating, enveloping the space between us with an almost suffocating aura.

Finally, he grips my hand with a firm squeeze. "I've heard a lot about you," Viper says, a smirk playing at the corners of his lips. My heart thunders in my chest as he continues. "You came to my compound drunk, puking in my flowers." He raises an eyebrow, daring me to deny the accusation.

Fuck.

My mind races, scrambling for a way to salvage the situation. "Oh, umm," I stammer, feeling like I'm floundering. I feel a flush of heat rise to my cheeks. The memory of that night is a source of deep embarrassment, and hearing it brought up now makes my throat dry up. "Uh, yeah, that was me," I manage, my voice coming out more as a croak than a statement.

"Classy Creed," Candi snorts as she walks up to stand beside me. I shoot her a glare. She was the one who supplied me with the alcohol and encouraged me to go win Vaughn back. But the look I give her goes unnoticed as her and Viper's gazes connect, the energy between them crackling like a live wire.

"You must be Candice Huxley," Viper says. A soft purr emanates from him, and my eyes widen in surprise as I volley my gaze between my best friend and my beta's uncle.

Candi shivers slightly, her posture suddenly more rigid. Her chin rises defiantly, and she looks Viper dead in the eye. "Candi," she corrects, her tone sharp. "Candice sounds like an old grandma name. And the only one allowed to call me that is my brother."

A deep chuckle vibrates through Viper, but there's a flicker of something darker in his eyes, a glimmer of challenge that matches Candi's defiance. "Whatever you say, sweetheart. It's a pleasure to meet you."

Candi blushes. Actually fucking blushes. Her cheeks turn a shade of pink that's hard to miss, and her usual sharp demeanor softens in a way that I've never seen before.

What the fuck is happening!?

CHAPTER 6
Creed

I'M SO STUNNED BY the interaction that I almost miss Vaughn descending the stairs. I startle as he speaks, my nerves fraying further. "Knock it off, Unc," Vaughn says, his warm palm resting on the back of my neck.

His touch is a comforting contrast to the tension in the room. My shoulders sag in relief as I glance up at Vaughn, then back at Viper. The older man's stoic expression remains unreadable, making me wonder if he already harbors a grudge against me.

But then, after an agonizingly slow moment, Viper bursts into laughter. The laughter from Viper seems genuine, but I can't shake the unease that still lingers. He claps me on the shoulder with enough force to make me wince, and I grit my teeth against the pain, forcing a strained smile.

The stocky guy next to Viper finally speaks up. "Don't pay our prez no mind. He's just busting your balls, son." The older man grins toothily. "I'm the tech genius around here. Name's Pixie."

Pixie?

The name strikes me as absurd given the guy's bulldog build—broad shoulders, a thick neck, and arms that could probably crush rocks. The irony is not lost on me, and I have to bite the inside of my cheek to suppress a laugh. Maybe that's the point.

"Nice to meet you, Pixie," I say, forcing a relaxed tone. Though the humor isn't lost on me I'm not in a joking mood right now. Pixie's grin widens, clearly accustomed to the reaction his name provokes.

"Likewise," Pixie replies, giving me a hearty slap on the back that nearly knocks the wind out of me. "So, you're the one who's got Vaughn all lovesick, huh? Must be something special."

I glance at Vaughn, who is barely containing his amusement. He gives me a subtle wink, which makes me feel a little better. "Ignore them, love. They're just trying to get under your skin. And Pix here is all bark," Vaughn murmurs into my ear.

The reassurance helps, and I feel a fraction of the tension ease. "Well, they're doing a great job," I mutter, earning another laugh from Pixie and Viper.

Fucking alphas.

As Viper's laughter dies down, his gaze shifts back to me, a glimmer of amusement still in his eyes. His dark stare turns back to Candi's and a subtle hitch catches in her throat at his attention, leaving me frowning. I'm unsure how I feel about my best friend being interested in the Steel Serpent MC president.

Viper's attention snaps back to Vaughn. "Where is Huxley? He told us to meet him here, and he didn't show?"

My anxiety spikes as I glance between Vaughn and Viper. I too am wondering where my alpha is as the uneasy silence stretches between us.

"Hux is making a connection with a few Hounds. It'll just be us meeting today," Vaughn answers, his tone clipped and neutral.

I frown. Hux isn't here? I bite the inside of my cheek, trying to hold back my frustration and focus on Viper.

Viper's gaze narrows on Vaughn, his voice dropping to a dangerous growl. "Why the fuck are you working with strays?"

Vaughn's nostrils flare with irritation. He hates that slur. It doesn't matter if Viper believes the Hounds are lowlifes, he knows calling them stray's will rub Vaughn the wrong way.

"We need to take back control of Sterling City, Unc. Some of the Hounds might be able to help with at least part of that."

"You can't honestly think you're going to win by recruiting from the slums? Not if you want our help, Vaughn. No. We don't work with Hounds." Viper steps closer to Vaughn, his tone hardening into a threat. "Ever."

Candi's eyes flash with anger, her stance defiant as she steps forward. "You have no idea what you're talking about. Just because you're the president of a little motorcycle club doesn't mean you're better than them. You don't get to come in here demanding *shit*, Viper."

Viper raises an eyebrow, clearly entertained by her defiance. "You're the one asking for our help, *sweetheart*. We get to set the terms of that arrangement."

"Vaughn may trust you, but I don't," Candi growls, lifting her chin in defiance. "If you want to be a part of something that takes back control of Sterling City, then you're going to do it my way."

Pixie laughs, shaking his head with a mix of amusement and admiration. "Damn, prez. Don't mess with the feisty omega."

"All you alphas are the same," Candi retorts, her eyes narrowing at Pixie.

Pixie steps closer, invading her space in an attempt to intimidate. But Candi stands her ground. They're almost eye level, with Pixie only a few inches taller. There's tension between her and the older alpha as they stare each other down. A silent struggle of wills. She narrows her eyes at him, and Pixie's smile widens approvingly.

"You really aren't afraid of us, are you?" Pixie asks, his tone almost admiring.

"Afraid of you? Why would I be afraid of you?"

Before Pixie can respond, Ghost's voice booms from across the bar, slicing through the tension with a commanding authority. "Enough."

I almost forgot he was here.

I watch him casually cross the bar toward us. His presence is overwhelming, the air around him crackling with his dominance. His eyes sweep the room, missing nothing.

"Who are you saying we should trust?" Ghost demands, his gaze locked with Candi's. "If you don't trust us, why should we trust your judgment?"

I startle at the force of his gaze, my instincts urging me to submit to his dominant presence. His green eyes flick to me momentarily, and I unconsciously take a step back, the intensity of his stare almost suffocating. My back hits Vaughn's chest and his chocolaty scent calms me slightly.

Vaughn clears his throat, answering in a steadier voice. "You should trust me, Ghost. You know *me*. And I'm telling you, Shade Jacobs has a plan to take out Titus. But for now we need to give a safe space to omegas. Everything in our city is going to shit and they deserve that much."

The two best friends have a stare off as my mind reels with this information, and I find myself blurting, "Shade? Kaylani's foster brother?" As my eyes narrow at Vaughn over my shoulder.

Vaughn nods, and a pang of frustration bubbles in my gut. There's more to Hux's plan than I'm being told, and I don't like being left in the dark by my pack.

"Fuck no. I'm not working with Shade," Viper snaps, his gaze flicking between Vaughn and Ghost. His jaw is clenched, and the tension in the room is almost unbearable, thick and heavy.

I let out a breath, exchanging a worried look with Candi. Her brows are furrowed, her expression a mix of determination and frustration. She needs this place most of all.

Before I can second-guess myself, I find my voice. And hope I'm right, that there is something going on between my best friend and the Serpents president. "Candi is unmated. Well, so am I... But not for long," I say, glancing briefly at Vaughn. "Kay and I won't be registering with the sanctuary, I can guarantee that. But Candi? I'm not sure what other options we have for her. She *needs* The Omega Den." I turn my attention back to Viper, hoping I'm not wrong and his instinct will be to protect her. "She will have to register with Bramwell along with all other unmated omegas in Sterling. It will be mandatory before long."

The room falls into a heavy silence and Viper's expression shifts, a mix of anger and calculation crossing his face. He turns his gaze to Candi and steps closer, his voice dropping to a soft, probing whisper.

"Do you want that, sweetheart? To give the Bramwell Sanctuary control over your scent match?" His eyes bore into hers, a dangerous curiosity glinting in their depths.

The thought of Candi being manipulated and controlled by the Sanctuary sends a shiver down my spine.

Candi's eyes narrow, her resolve unwavering. "No one will choose my pack for me, Viper," she snaps, her voice carrying a challenge. "And that includes you."

Viper's lips curl into a faint smirk, but there's a dark edge to his smile. "I respect that," he says quietly. "You shouldn't have your future dictated for you, sweetheart. But I'm curious."

He tilts his head, his gaze sweeping down her frame with a predatory glint. "You're perfuming. Is it for me? Ghost? It damn sure isn't for Pixie."

I realize with a jolt that Viper is essentially asking if she's attracted to him, if she's considering him as an option.

Candi's lips twitch into a sardonic smile, her arms crossing over her chest. "Are you going to help us or not, Viper?" she demands, her voice cutting through the charged silence with a sharp edge.

She's not backing down, her defiance clear despite the undercurrent of tension between them. The air crackles with anticipation, as if the room itself is waiting for Viper's response. He glances back at Ghost, who gives a subtle nod.

"Yes, Candi," Viper finally says, his voice soft but firm. "I'll help you, but under one condition."

He steps closer to her, his gaze intense and unwavering. "I want you as my omega."

Candi's eyes widen in disbelief, her mouth slightly open as she absorbs his words. "You've got to be fucking kidding me. You think you can just waltz in here and make demands like that?"

Viper's expression remains serious, his gaze unyielding. "Consider this, sweetheart. You need protection and a secure place to call home. Your brother will soon have a pack of his own and the Bramwell Sanctuary won't offer what you need. Plus, I'll let you choose any of my men to bond with—hell, claim them all if you want. I just want to be first."

"Let me choose who I want," she scoffs, a shiver of discomfort running through her. "And why would I ever consider becoming some omega slut?"

Viper's smirk widens, clearly confident in his offer. "You're already thinking about it," he says with a soft chuckle.

His voice drops to a whisper.. "Here's the deal. Agree to at least consider being mine, and I'll help you with your club." His fingers brush her hair over her shoulder..

I stifle a snort, watching as Candi's sharp, calculating gaze shifts to me. Her expression is a mix of frustration and contemplation, clearly weighing her options.

Fuck. My best friend is totally screwed.

It's official—Candi Huxley has met her match.

CHAPTER 7

Kaylani

A s I sit on the front porch of my childhood home the cool breeze rustles the leaves, a gentle reminder of simpler times. I used to spend hours here, in this very spot. Lost in books or buried in homework. But today, the serenity of the porch offers little relief from the turmoil within me. Nausea rolls through my stomach, a cold sweat breaking out on my brow. I should take another dose of Heat to keep my instincts in check. I'm not ready for my heat. Especially since I can *feel* that this one is going to be different.

I take a shaky sip of my coffee, letting the warmth settle in my belly. But even my favorite drink does little to ease the fire under my skin. It feels like ants crawling beneath my flesh, each movement a sharp reminder that my heat is coming, whether I want it to or not. Fear grips me, twisting my stomach into knots.

The temptation to take another dose of the stimulant is almost overwhelming. Just one more hit to keep the heat at bay, to avoid the agony of coming off it cold turkey. Because even though I'm just a few days late taking it, my body is on fire.

The bottle I stole is sitting in my purse. It would be so easy to take one. To stop my heat from coming. But that thought is like a knife to my chest, a painful reminder of my mother. She let her hormones dictate her life, drowning in the cycle of addiction until it consumed her. I swore I'd never be like her. I'd never let myself fall into that same trap.

But knowing the worst heat of my life is on the horizon, knowing I'm not ready to face it, makes it so damn hard. Especially with Adam's bite still searing like a brand on my skin. My fingers trace the ridges on my shoulder, the mark he left there. The spot hums to life under my touch, and tears of frustration prick my eyes. My body is betraying me, craving something I despise, something I fear.

I take another sip of coffee, clutching the mug tightly to give my hands something to do. The warmth of the cup does little to ease the icy fear settling in my chest. I'm terrified—terrified of the way my body will soon crave Adam's knot, how the Heat will force me into a frenzied state where I might accept his touch if he's near. Maybe that's why I keep seeing glimpses of him in my peripheral vision, why his scent seems to linger on the breeze, and why his face haunts me even when I close my eyes.

I shiver, the sensation of his gaze on me almost palpable, though I know it's not possible. He's never been to Eden's house before—how could he possibly know I'm here? The thought of him here, in my safe space, sends a wave of revulsion through me, washing over me like a cold, unforgiving tide. I'm standing on the edge of a cliff, the icy abyss below calling to me, and the urge to leap is becoming harder to resist.

What's one more dose, really?

I close my eyes, taking a deep breath of the fresh summer breeze in an effort to calm the storm raging inside me. The scent of pine and earth fills my lungs, grounding me momentarily.

The front door creaks open, and I force a smile onto my face as Shade joins me on the porch swing. "Morning, Kay Kay," he greets, unaware of the battle raging within me. Thankfully the wind carries my perfumes away from him and he hasn't noticed my scent change. Yet.

We sit in silence, sipping our morning coffee. The gentle creak of the porch swing provides a soothing rhythm, blending with the sounds of birds greeting the day.

"I missed it here," I say, finally breaking the silence.

Shade nods, pushing the swing slightly with the balls of his feet. "Yeah, we've missed you around here," he agrees, his voice soft and reflective. "You should start coming to Sunday dinners again, Kay. It's not the same without you."

"Did I just hear you saying something nice?" I tease, a playful grin spreading across my face. "I'm in shock," I add, raising an eyebrow.

Shade isn't someone who normally gets all mushy about feelings. His brows furrow as he meets my gaze, but he quickly masks his features, forcing a chuckle that doesn't sound genuine. Something is definitely up with him.

He's hiding something.

"Don't get used to it," he warns, but there's a warmth in his eyes that wasn't there before and guilt settles in my stomach. Whatever he is hiding from me probably isn't my business. Plus aren't I hiding something from him too? From everyone? I study his face, trying to read between the lines.

"Shade, what's going on? You never get sentimental like this."

Shade hesitates, his usually confident demeanor slipping just enough for me to notice. He's not looking at me now, his gaze fixed on the horizon as if searching for the right words. The silence between us grows heavy, and I feel my heart start to race.

"Kay," he finally says, his voice unusually soft, almost fragile. "There's something I need to tell you."

I set my coffee cup down, my hands suddenly too shaky to hold it. "What is it?" I ask, dread curling in my stomach. Shade isn't one to hesitate like this. If he's holding back, it's bad.

Really bad.

He sighs, running a hand through his hair, a gesture so out of character that it spikes my anxiety even more. "I made a deal," he starts, his voice rough. "With Sean Cromwell."

My blood runs cold at the mention of that name.

Sean Cromwell isn't just any alpha—he's dangerous, cunning, ruthless. The kind of alpha who doesn't make deals unless he plans to collect. The Cromwell pack is feared for good reason, their reputation one of violence and cruelty. The mere thought of Sean Cromwell brings back memories of whispered warnings, of deals gone horribly wrong, of bodies that vanished without a trace. Whatever Shade has gotten himself into...

It's not good.

"Cromwell?" I repeat, my voice barely steady. "Shade, what kind of deal did you make with him?"

His eyes meet mine, and the guilt there is unmistakable. "I promised to help him become the new kingpin of the Hounds. And in exchange we'll get his help taking down Titus and securing the Den for omegas."

"Why not just tell Liam? He's a cop. He could put Titus away," I argue, desperation creeping into my voice. As I make the suggestion, I already know he would never get enough dirt on Titus to keep him in prison permanently. Especially with Michelle silently backing him.

Liam is Shade's best friend, a morally upstanding alpha. So no matter what he should be the logical choice here.

Shade shifts uncomfortably, his eyes flitting away from mine as if he can't bear to see the disappointment or fear he knows is there. The weight of his decision hangs between us like a dark cloud, thickening the air.

"Liam's a good alpha," Shade admits, his voice low and tense. "But good isn't enough. Titus is too well-connected, too entrenched in the city's underworld. Even if Liam could put him away, it wouldn't be permanent. Titus would find a way to slip through the cracks, and he'd come back angrier, more dangerous," he says what I've been thinking and a shiver travels up my spine.

Shade's words settle over me like a heavy weight, suffocating the hope I had clung to. Titus is a monster who thrives on power and fear, someone who has built an empire on the broken lives of others. And yet, the thought of aligning with Sean Cromwell, of helping him rise to power, feels like making a deal with the devil.

"Sean is an alpha of his word," Shade continues, his tone hardening as he forces himself to meet my gaze again. "He wants to be the kingpin of the Hounds, and he wants to rid the city of Heat. He sees it as a tool of control, something Titus uses to enslave others. He hates it as much as we do. If Cromwell rises to power, he'll cut off Titus's strength at the source. But he needs help to do it."

I swallow hard, trying to wrap my head around the twisted logic of this deal. On one hand, getting rid of Heat might actually save lives, free omegas from the grip of their worst instincts. On the other hand, it's *Sean-fucking-Cromwell*. There's no telling what kind of world he'll shape if he succeeds in becoming kingpin.

"So, what?" I ask, my voice trembling with barely contained fear. "Are you going to pledge to the Hounds now? Swear loyalty to Cromwell and become one of his enforcers? A Hound?"

Shade's reaction is immediate, his face hardening with a mix of anger and regret. "No, Kay. I'm not pledging to anyone. This is a business arrangement, nothing more. I'm doing what needs to be done to protect us, to protect Sterling. But I'll never be one of Cromwell's dogs."

"But it doesn't work like that, Shade!" I snap, unable to keep the fear and frustration out of my voice. "Once Cromwell gets his claws into you he's not going to just let you walk away. He's going to want more, demand more. And what happens when you can't give it to him? Or when he turns on you like he's done to so many others?"

His silence is deafening. He's made his choice, but that doesn't make it any less terrifying. He might think he can walk away from Cromwell unscathed, but deep down, we both know it's not that simple.

"I just hope you know what you're doing," I say, my voice barely above a whisper. "Because once you let someone like Sean in, there's no going back."

Shade doesn't respond, his gaze locked on the horizon as if searching for answers that aren't there. And in that moment, I realize just how far he's willing to go to protect the people he loves. He'll do whatever it takes, even if it means walking into the lion's den.

A familiar, gnawing temptation resurfaces as my worries grow. I think about the heat stimulant, the one thing that has been my crutch through all of this. The thought of taking another dose seems more alluring than ever. Put off dealing with my heat until things calm down in my life.

What's one more dose? Just one more time. Avoid my heat for one more cycle.

I'm not sure if I'll be able to keep from falling off the edge. The cliff is no longer just a metaphor. It's a looming, tangible threat, and the darkness below is growing ever more enticing.

CHAPTER 8

Kaylani

H UX'S SEDAN PULLS UP in front of the house, its engine purring
softly before falling silent. He steps out of the car, closing the
door with a gentle click. His hair is cut short, and peppered beard neatly
trimmed to match. Though I've always preferred his beard longer. I recall
how it scratches my soft skin when he kisses me, shivering at the memory.

My eyes trail down his muscular frame, taking in every detail as though he's
a refreshing drink on a scorching day. The dark suit he wears is impeccably
tailored, accentuating his broad shoulders and adding a layer of sophisti-
cation to his striking presence. Despite his polished appearance, there's a
rugged edge to Hux that makes my heart race. I think about the tattoos
that hide beneath that sleek suit, and my gaze snaps back to his face where
a smirk plays on his lips.

Damn, he's gorgeous.

His eyes, sharp and assessing, lock onto mine as he strides toward the porch with purpose. I can't tear my gaze away. I'm like a moth to a flame, suddenly forgetting why I was so furious with him.

"What are you doing here?" I ask, my voice breathier than I'd intended.

"You didn't think I would come find you, kitten? You left me. Of course I'd come looking for you," he replies smoothly, the smirk never fading. "Thanks for the call, man." His gaze shifts to Shade with an almost amused detachment.

"Call? You called him, Shade?" I exclaim, spinning to face my brother. Shock and anger collide within me, and I smack him on the back of the head. "What the hell!"

"Ow! Don't hit me, Kay Kay. Not nice," Shade grumbles, rubbing the spot where I smacked him. I snort at his exaggerated pout.

"Traitor," I mutter, though there's no real malice in my tone.

"You love me, Kay Kay," Shade says with a grin that only broadens. "And yeah, I called him. He's your alpha."

"He's not my alpha—" I start to protest, my frustration bubbling over.

"I'm not your alpha, kitten?" Hux's voice cuts in, sharp and challenging. The dark, possessive edge to his tone sends a shiver down my spine. His spicy scent washes over me like a tidal wave, igniting a firestorm of heat that courses through my veins, leaving me trembling with need. My body responds instinctively to his proximity, the slick running down my thighs an act of betrayal.

"I... umm." My mind feels like it's short-circuiting, the words getting stuck in my throat as I struggle to form a coherent response. His nostrils flare as he catches the scent of my perfume.

I glare at him. The effect he has on me isn't fair.

It's just the drugs talking. He couldn't possibly want me.

I'm too broken and damaged.

The little monster of self-doubt whispers in my head and I shake the thought away. No, it's not just that, he is my scent match. Memories of that night back at the Den filter through my mind and I know that he is the alpha I want. Not Adam.

"I'm supposed to be mad at you," I say, lifting my chin in defiance.

I'm about two seconds away from jumping his bones.

"I'll leave you two lovebirds alone," Shade says, slipping back into the house. But I can't even respond as Hux's low growl vibrates through me, the sound making my core throb with need.

FUCK.

"Are you going to come home willingly, kitten?" Hux's voice cuts through the haze of desire. "Or do I need to toss you over my shoulder?"

His blue eyes pierce mine with an intensity that sends a shiver down my spine, stirring something primal within me. I struggle to maintain my composure, to resist the overwhelming urge to surrender to the pleasure that threatens to consume me. But it's a losing battle, like trying to hold back a flood with nothing but my bare hands. Every fiber of my being screams for release, for the comfort and relief that only an alpha can provide.

Only Hux can provide.

"Hux," I manage to whisper, my voice barely audible above the roaring of my blood in my ears.

As he steps closer, an agonizing pain I've never felt before engulfs me like wildfire. It spreads through my limbs like scalding lava, and a blinding white-hot flash bursts across my vision. Every nerve in my body feels as if it's on fire, each breath coming in jagged gasps, like shards of glass scraping against my lungs. Tears blur my sight as I clench my fists, struggling to endure the relentless waves of heat crashing over me.

"Kitten?" Hux asks softly, his hand brushing along my arm. I cry out in pain, the touch intensifying the searing heat coursing through me.

"Don't," I beg, my voice cracking with agony. "Please, don't touch me."

Hux's eyes widen with concern as he retracts his hand, but his gaze remains fixed on me, a mix of worry and something else burning in his blue eyes. He steps back, giving me space, but the air between us crackles with unspoken tension.

"What's happening to you?" His voice is rough, a touch of desperation seeping through as he takes in my pained expression.

Lie. My inner voice prompts.

"I—I don't know." The lie tastes bitter on my tongue. Even as my heat overwhelms me, I can't bring myself to face the look of disappointment he would give me if he knew I had been willingly taking the stimulant. And that I would have again today if he hadn't shown up. I gasp, each breath sending a sharp zing down to my core.

"Kay, is it your heat?" Hux asks as he crouches before me, his eyes filled with anguish. "What can I do, kitten? How do I help you?"

The raw concern in his voice brings tears to my eyes. Guilt swirls inside me, a vortex of self-recrimination. But amid the torment, there's a dangerous part of me that craves Hux's touch, that's yearning for the comfort and relief only he can provide. The temptation is perilous, threatening to consume me entirely if I let it.

"Just... just stay with me," I manage to whisper. "Don't leave me alone."

Hux's expression softens, and he moves closer again, though he respects the distance I've asked for. "I'm not going anywhere," he purrs softly. "Tell me what you need."

I close my eyes, focusing on the rumble in his chest, the soothing sound of his purr diminishing some of the pain. With a trembling hand, I reach out to him. Hux frowns, but slowly brushes his fingertips along mine.

I whimper again, my eyes clouding with tears.

"Fuck," He growls. The frustration in his voice makes me want to soothe him, my omega instinct vying for control.

As the tears stream down my face, clearing my blurred vision, Hux's bright blue eyes come into focus. I see the moment realization dawns on him. His beautiful face morphs into something dark—sharp and hard.

Rage.

I whimper, the intensity of his spicy scent wrapping around me. His jaw clenches, a fierce possessiveness flashing across his features as the truth sinks in. "Did you take it?" he demands, his voice cutting through the air with an accusatory edge. We both know exactly what he means by *it*.

I can't bear to meet his gaze, the force of his disappointment feeling like an unbearable weight pressing down on me.

"Answer me," he barks, his tone a commanding hiss. He didn't yell it at me in the slightest and that somehow makes the situation feel even worse.

"I'm sorry," I sob, the words barely escaping through my tears. "I didn't mean to... at first," I whisper, my voice trembling. "Don't hate me, Hux. I couldn't bear it if you hated me."

His expression falters, caught between anger and something deeper. For a moment, he just stares at me, his fury blending with a profound sadness that cuts through the rage. The intensity of his silence amplifies my sense of desperation, magnifying my feeling of loss. Tears continue to fall in silent streams down my cheeks.

He hates me, and I don't blame him.

Hux's hand reaches out tentatively, his fingers a hair's breadth from touching my cheek before he withdraws, letting his hand fall to his side.

"I don't hate you. I could *never* hate you," he says, his voice filled with an aching gentleness. "But why didn't you tell me, kitten?"

I clench my thighs together, trying to stem the ache coursing through me.

"Like you told me about the Hounds," I counter, my voice strained and defensive. The accusation lingers in the air between us, a painful reminder of the secrets that we both have been keeping and the trust that is broken.

Hux's shoulders sag slightly as he crouches in front of me.

"I didn't know the full extent of Titus's plan, kitten, *I swear it*. All I knew was that Michelle wanted your bond with Adam broken and Candice to take your place," he admits quietly, his voice heavy with regret. "I should have told you. I'm sorry. I wanted to protect you. I see now. But don't let my mistake make you suffer more than you already have. You shouldn't have had to face this alone."

"I didn't want to bother you," I mumble, my cheeks flushing with embarrassment.

He moves to one knee in front of me, bringing our faces inches apart. His eyes darken with an intensity that makes my heart race. "Bother me?" he murmurs. "You think your heat is a bother to me?"

I open my mouth to respond, but his proximity, the heat surging through me, and the intensity in his gaze make coherent thought nearly impossible. His breath skims my skin, hot and tantalizing, causing me to whimper helplessly.

"You're mine, Kaylani," he growls, his voice a low, rumbling declaration that seems to resonate deep within my core. "There is nothing you could *ever* do that would make me not want you."

I try to speak, but the intensity of his gaze and the strength of my heat render me mute. All I can do is give him a watery smile. My mind, body, and soul are overwhelmed with his promises and scent.

I don't deserve someone like him.

"I'll call Creed. He'll know how to handle this. I didn't realize you were going through this alone." Hux's voice is a soothing balm amid the chaos, but I look away, unable to meet his gaze. After a moment he sighs and steps away. The shame of my actions threatens to pull me deeper into an abyss of self-recrimination. I shouldn't be burdening him with my choices.

I hear his footsteps on the porch as his sandalwood scent engulfs me once more. "Kitten, I need to pick you up, get you home. Creed and Vaughn are waiting for us." His hands make contact with my shoulders and a searing pain rips a scream from my throat. The intensity of his alpha presence overwhelms my senses, sending waves of agony crashing over me like a relentless tide.

Every nerve in my body feels like it's on fire, my skin burning with an unbearable intensity. The pain is excruciating, a relentless assault that threatens to consume me whole. I gasp for breath, my chest heaving as I cling to his shoulders, desperate for any reprieve from the torment coursing through my veins.

"Hux," I choke out, my voice cracking with the desperate plea. "Please... it hurts..."

"Almost there, kitten. Hang on, baby. Breathe in and out through your mouth," he instructs.

I writhe in his grasp, struggling to follow his instructions as the waves of pain threaten to overwhelm me.

"You can do this," Hux murmurs, his voice a gentle purr that contrasts with the fierce intensity of his earlier tone. "Just hang on. You're such a good girl."

His purr rattles softly. "Let's get you home so your pack can take care of you," he says firmly. Carefully, he sets me in the backseat of his sedan.

"Hurts," I manage to whisper, my voice barely more than a breath.

"I know, baby. Rest," he commands softly, his alpha bark weaving into the command, offering a semblance of calm amidst the storm.

I settle into the leather seat, my eyes closing at his alpha bark. Despite everything, I trust Hux to guide me through the darkness that slowly engulfs me.

CHAPTER 9

Kaylani

T HE PAIN IS EXCRUCIATING, as if someone took a red-hot poker, plunged it into the fire, and then pierced my flesh with it. I cry out as another wave of slick rushes down my thighs. A cold sweat breaks out on my forehead, and my clothes feel suffocating. Desperation takes over as I begin to blindly claw at my sweat-soaked garments, trying to rip them off.

Vaughn appears above me, his lips are moving, but I can't make out anything he is saying. My heart pounds in my ears, drowning out all other sounds. He glances over his shoulder as he speaks and there's tension in his jaw that I want to smooth away. I fixate on the spot between his brows, which are pinched with concern as his dark gaze locks onto me again, and I feel a pang of guilt for making my pack worry.

"Hurts," I mumble through chattering teeth, the intensity of the pain making me fear I'll break a tooth.

Strong hands help wrench my clothes off over my head and I let them, grateful for the help. The scent of coffee envelops me, my pack's scents all mingling together in a delicious blend that triggers another wave of pleasure to course through my core with such intensity that I curl into myself, gasping for air.

"Take her to the bathroom," Hux barks, his voice cutting through the haze of pain with a commanding force. I'm swept up into strong arms and the sudden movement sends another groan of pain through me.

"Don't worry, doll, I got you," Vaughn reassures me, his voice a soothing balm against the storm raging inside me.

"Make it stop," I beg, my voice trembling with agony. The plea is a raw, desperate cry that seems to hang in the air, unanswered.

"You're okay, tiny," Creed's voice comes from somewhere behind me, but I can't turn to look at him. Instead, I bury my face into Vaughn's neck, seeking comfort in his warm, chocolaty scent. His beta scent grounds, soothing the intense fire roaring through me to a dull ache. The scents of the others seem to send my hormones into a frenzy, intensifying the pain and confusion.

Vaughn's body is tense as he carries me toward the bathroom. Every jolt from his movements sends another spike of pain shooting through me, and I whimper, clutching at him desperately. The scent of coffee with a hint of sweet caramel from Creed, and the subtle undertone of sandalwood and spice from Hux fill my senses.

It's all too much.

My mind is a whirlwind of sensation, each one pulling me in a different direction until I feel like I'm being torn apart from the inside out. I whimper, burying my nose into Vaughn's chest and inhaling his scent greedily.

"I know, doll. Just hold on a little longer," Vaughn murmurs, his voice strained with the effort of trying to keep me calm.

But his words barely register. All I can focus on is the relentless fire raging beneath my skin, the unbearable need clawing at my insides, demanding release.

As we enter the bathroom, the cooler air hits my overheated skin, offering a brief moment of relief before it's swallowed up by the next wave of heat. I cling to Vaughn, my nails digging into his shoulders as if holding on to him will keep me from being swept away by the storm inside me.

"Hux, get the tub ready," Creed orders, his voice calm. It's unlike the goofy omega I've come to know. There's a sense of urgency beneath his tone that terrifies me.

Hux's presence, even from across the room, is enough to trigger another wave of slick to coat my thighs, my body reacting instinctively to my alpha. Vaughn's grip tightens on me, and I can taste the subtle hint of frustration in his scent.

"Hux, leave," Vaughn growls. "You're only making it worse."

I feel a pang of guilt as Creed pushes Hux toward the door, but deep down, I know he's right.

The air hitting my sensitive skin sends shivers through me. The smallest movement, even the faintest touch of air, intensifies my pleasure. My clit throbs, pussy clamping down around nothing. I've never been more desperate for release.

I whimper as I'm drowning in a sea of sensation.

As Vaughn carries me toward the tub, I cling to him, hoping that once I'm submerged in the water the storm inside me will finally be calmed.

I'm not sure how much more I can take.

"We need to get your temperature down, tiny," Creed says, his voice closer now. I nod weakly, my head rattling with the small movement, nausea swirling inside my belly.

"Vaughn, get her into the tub."

Vaughn lowers us carefully into the icy water, and it feels like I'm sitting on pins and needles. I cry out in agony as the freezing water seeps into my pores. His movements are slow and deliberate, as if any sudden shift might break me or send me crashing over the edge.

To be honest, it might.

I whimper as the cold water settles around us. But even as the cold numbs some of the pain, the need for release still gnaws at me, relentless and unforgiving. I cling to Vaughn, my fingers curling into his shirt as if he's the only thing keeping me tethered to reality.

"I'm sorry," I whisper, my voice breaking. But Vaughn only shakes his head, his expression softening as he cups my face in his hands.

"Don't apologize, doll. We're going to take care of you, okay?," he murmurs, his thumb brushing away the tears I didn't even realize were falling.

I nod, too exhausted to do anything else. I can feel Creed's hand on my shoulder, his presence a steady, grounding force beside me.

"We've got you, tiny," Creed says, his voice firm. "You're not alone. We're here. Pass her to me," he demands, as he climbs into the tub beside me, fully clothed.

Gently, Vaughn shifts me into Creed's waiting arms, the water sloshing with their movements. The cold water soaks through their clothes, but neither seems to care as they focus on comforting me.

I nestle into Creed's chest, my back to his front. His arms wrap around me protectively. A fresh wave of need courses through me and I cry out in surprise at the sudden force of it.

"M-make it s-stop," I plead, my voice trembling, my teeth biting into my tongue as I try to speak. The taste of copper floods my mouth, but I can barely focus on it over the overwhelming need tearing through me.

Slowly, Creed's fingers slide between my thighs, finding my overly sensitive clit with practiced ease. His touch is gentle but insistent, his fingers moving in quick, measured circles that send jolts of pleasure through my ravaged body.

"Let go tiny," Creed murmurs into my ear.

The demand has me crying out, the sound raw and desperate as the pleasure overtakes me, and I'm crashing over the edge within seconds. The world around me blurs as I'm propelled into a realm of pure sensation, stars exploding behind my eyelids as relief floods through me.

My body sags against Creed, trembling, as he rocks me back and forth, helping me ride out the last, shuddering wave of pleasure. His touch is soothing, his murmured words of comfort barely registering as I try to catch my breath.

"Sleep baby girl, I'm not going anywhere."

CHAPTER 10
Kaylani

WHEN I FINALLY MANAGE to open my eyes, they settle on Vaughn, who's sitting across from me in the tub. His clothes are drenched, clinging to his broad shoulders like a second skin, and water drips down the hard lines of his jaw. His onyx gaze is so intense and filled with hunger that it stokes the fire inside me back to life with fierce, consuming heat.

I suck in a sharp breath and his scent captivates me, pulling a soft moan from my lips. The air thickens with my perfume—fresh-cut roses that mingle with the bitter sweetness of my pack's combined scents.

The aroma is dizzying.

My eyes follow the path of water down Vaughn's temple, tracing the sharp curve of his jaw and onto his neck. The urge to taste him surges through me, overwhelming and insistent. My mouth waters with the desperate, needy ache to taste him—to lick and suck every last drop of the desire I see mirrored in his onyx eyes.

"Do you taste like chocolate?" the words slip out in a breathy whisper. The moment the question leaves my lips my eyes widen in shock, and a deep flush spreads across my cheeks. Vaughn's gaze darkens, his eyes flashing with something raw and primal. He leans in slightly, the water sloshing over the edge of the tub.

"What was that, doll?"

I bite my lip, the weight of my own desire making my heart race.

"I-I didn't mean to say that out loud," I stammer, my embarrassment only fueling the heat that pulses between us. But the look in Vaughn's eyes tells me there's no taking it back now, and a shiver runs through me as I realize just how much he enjoyed hearing it.

Vaughn's lips curve into a slow, wicked smile. "Oh, I think you did," he murmurs, his voice dripping with dark promise. "And now that you've said it... there's no going back."

I swallow hard, my heart pounding in my chest. "I... I want to taste you," I stammer, the words tumbling out in a rush before I can second-guess myself.

A slow, wicked smile spreads across Vaughn's face, his hunger barely restrained as he watches me squirm under the weight of my own desires. "You're playing with fire, doll," he murmurs, his voice a rough caress that sends a shiver down my spine. "But if that's what you want..."

The air between us thickens with tension. Vaughn's presence is overwhelming, his drenched form so close yet still just out of reach. My body reacts instinctively, a fresh wave of slick rushing between my thighs, my scent spiking. The delicate aroma of roses fills the small, steamy space, mingling with the heady mix of coffee and spice that clings to Vaughn's skin.

I can't tear my gaze away from him, the sight of Vaughn drenched and dripping, his hunger now fully unleashed, drives me to the edge of my control. "I need you, Vaughn," I whisper, the confession tumbling out of me in a desperate plea. "Please..."

Creed's hand slides up my stomach, his touch soothing as he whispers instructions to Vaughn. "Go set up a nest in my room downstairs. She's going to have another wave soon and we need to prepare her," he instructs softly, his deep voice vibrating against my ear as he continues to comfort me. The calmness in his tone is a stark contrast to the tension thrumming through his body, a controlled urgency as he tries to prepare for the next inevitable onslaught of heat.

Vaughn hesitates, his gaze locked on mine, his jaw tightening as if he's fighting against the pull between us. Finally, he nods, the tension in his broad shoulders visible as he stands. Water streams off his clothes, glistening on his tattoos, and as he pushes his damp hair back with a hand, the sight of droplets trailing down his muscled arms makes my breath hitch. The urge to lean forward and lick each bead of water off his skin is nearly unbearable, a primal instinct that claws at my restraint.

But Vaughn forces himself to step out of the tub, leaving me trembling in Creed's arms, his presence a burning imprint that refuses to fade even as he disappears from view. The loss of him leaves me aching, the need still pulsing through me, but Creed's firm, steady hold is enough to keep me grounded—for now.

Creed tilts my chin up to face him, his expression pinched with worry as he searches my eyes. "We're going to get through this, okay?"

I nod weakly.

"About a year ago, my mother dosed me with Heat," he confesses, his voice low and filled with sadness.

"Creed–"

"Shh," he interrupts my attempt to speak. "Please, Kay, just listen. This is important. The pain will come back, and I'm so sorry about that, but you need to be prepared." His bright green eyes lock onto mine through the strands of his overgrown hair plastered to his forehead, his expression a blend of worry and determination.

My stomach sinks.

"Come back?" I ask, my voice cracking with fear.

He nods. "I wish I could take it away from you, but I can't. For now, just relax and try to rest. Vaughn and I will be here for you every step of the way." His eyes search mine, seeking reassurance. "You know that... don't you?" His thumb gently rubs soothing circles on my jaw.

I nod. I trust that Vaughn and Creed will be here for me.

"Yes." Closing my eyes, I allow myself to sink into his hold, relaxing against his chest.

Creed clears his throat, the sound rough and jagged, as if he's trying to dislodge something stuck inside. "I should warn you, the heat that hit me was..." he pauses as if looking for the right words.

"The most painful experience of my life. It felt like I would die without a knot, but when I finally had one... it was with an alpha my mother had set up for me." His hands tremble as he speaks. "But remember everything you've been through, tiny. You're strong. You'll be okay."

I move to turn back to face him, but his arms tighten around my chest, holding me still. "Once the medication finally wore off," Creed continues, his voice now a whisper, "I think it was about three days later. I came here. To Vaughn. And I never looked back." His words linger in the air, heavy with the weight of his past and the pain that still haunts him.

My fists clench, nails digging into my palms as anger surges through me. The thought of Creed being forced through this makes my blood boil and my stomach churn with rage. Panic grips my chest, tightening around my heart like a vice.

Three days of agonizing heat?

The thought alone is unbearable. I couldn't—wouldn't—survive something like that.

Finally, he lets me turn to face him. The sorrow in his eyes, the regret—it's the same look he had when Vaughn broke their bond. But beyond that, I see his strength, the resolve that carried him through his own hell. He survived it. Maybe I can too.

His thumb brushes over my lower lip with tender strokes. "I was so fucking mad at you for leaving the funeral, tiny," he says, his voice raw and strained. Guilt gnaws at my insides, twisting painfully. I was so overwhelmed by Hux hiding things from me that I ran, but hearing Creed's anguish brings that hurt into sharper focus.

"I never meant to hurt you," I admit, my voice barely above a whisper.

He sighs heavily, his eyes searching mine as if pleading for understanding. "I was forced to walk away from Vaughn once. Remember? It nearly broke me. But if I lost you…"

The gravity of his words settles over me, making my chest tighten. The memory of Creed's shattered expression when Vaughn broke their bond is etched into my mind. The thought of causing him that kind of pain again is unbearable. I lean into his touch, pressing a kiss into his palm, trying to convey all the regret and sorrow I feel at bringing up those feelings for him again by walking away.

"I'm sorry, Creed," I say, my voice trembling.

Creed's gaze softens slightly. "Do you not understand that I love you? That I'm yours? Please don't ever run from me. *Please*," he begs.

My heart aches at the raw honesty in his voice. I know I have a habit of running when things get tough, but seeing the impact it has on him is a wake-up call.

"I love you too," I whisper, my heart swelling with the realization.

Creed's hand smooths across my jaw, and I can feel the tremor in his touch. "Promise me you won't leave me, Kaylani," he pleads, using my full name instead of his nickname for me. "Promise me you won't run from me again. I need to know you'll stay and face this with me. All this shit around us is bearable if I have my pack. If I have you."

The intensity in his gaze makes my heart pound. I can see the depth of his vulnerability, and it cuts through me like a knife. The fear in his eyes—fear of losing me, fear of being alone again—makes me realize how much I mean to him.

I nod. "I promise," I murmur, and then his lips capture mine.

CHAPTER 11
Kaylani

T HE DISORIENTATION IS OVERWHELMING. For a moment, I forget where I am as the world spins in a haze. Adam's haunting green eyes flash in my vision, my body vibrating with a desperate craving I don't want. I whimper, squeezing my eyes shut against the intrusive thoughts. "I would never want you, Adam," I grit out through clenched teeth.

"Shh, tiny," Creed's voice cuts through the fog. I'm adrift in warm water, Creed's arms around me, his presence anchoring me as I focus on the smooth porcelain of the bathtub. "We're getting you through this. Your second wave is coming. You can handle it."

I nod, though doubt gnaws at me. Another wave of heat crashes over me before I can brace myself, tears streaming down my cheeks as the pain flares up, burning me from the inside out. It feels unbearable, the pain fogging my mind and making it hard to think. Through the haze I glimpse Hux standing at the door. His eyes lock on mine, a blend of longing and regret in their icy blue depths. My heart seizes in my chest, my omega instincts going haywire. But before I can reach out or call to him, Creed's voice slices through the silence.

"Hux, I know you care about her and your instincts are telling you to soothe our omega. But right now your scent is only making it more painful for her. You need to trust that Vaughn and I will take care of her. Trust your pack, alpha."

Hux's gaze flits between Creed and me, his expression torn. This is the first time Creed has ever called him alpha, and I can see it soothes some of his alpha instincts.

"I'm sorry, kitten," he says, his voice thick with emotion. "I shouldn't have come, but I needed to check on you. It's been hours, and I was worried."

I try to muster a smile, to reassure him that I'm okay, but the intensity of the pain traps the words in my throat. His look of horror is almost unbearable to see. I know he would never mean to cause me harm. Hux takes a step back, retreating from the room with a shamed expression pinching his brows.

"Forgive me," he whispers before disappearing from view.

Tears cloud my eyes, blurring the figure of Vaughn's standing in the doorway. His presence is a comforting anchor amidst the chaos. "The nest is ready, doll."

"Get her a towel love," Creed instructs as he rises from the now lukewarm water, cradling me in his strong arms.

Vaughn quickly retrieves a towel, wrapping the soft fabric around me, but the sensation is unbearable, like ants crawling across my skin. I whimper, the discomfort almost too much to bear. Vaughn's hand is gentle as it brushes away my tears.

"Hang on to me, doll," he murmurs, his voice a soft plea that cuts through the haze clouding my mind. He sweeps me up bridal style and I turn my face into his chest, my jaw locking tightly as an intense wave of heat crashes over me. My mouth waters as I pant through the overwhelming sensation, my body craving something I can't quite grasp. Following instincts, I lick up the base of Vaughn's neck, a low, throaty moan vibrating in my chest. The taste of his skin is intoxicating, sending a shock of pleasure straight to my core.

"Careful, doll," he croaks as his fingers dig into my hip, holding me securely in his arms as he carries me down the corridor. I haven't paid much attention to where he's taking me—I'm focused on only one thing.

The urge to suck, to bite, to mark my beta.

It's all-consuming, a primal need roaring to life within me. The scent of him wraps around me, pulling me deeper into a feral heat that blurs the line between need and sanity.

"Mine," I growl against his fluttering pulse, nuzzling into his neck and pressing my scent into him, claiming him. A purr vibrates in my chest, and I can smell my own perfume—rich and intoxicating—filling the air around us. It's stronger than ever, potent and overwhelming, feeding the frenzy inside me. My bitter scent clings to him, mingling with his sweat and musk, driving my need to claim him even higher.

Is this how Adam felt?

The thought slices through the haze, sharp and cold, and I gasp, a chilling dread piercing the heat as the memory of Adam's bite flares to life. He had bitten me, forced his mark on me, but I had refused to bite him in return. It had driven him mad, feral, leaving him lost to the instincts that had consumed him. Was he drugged like me? Like Creed was?

My own bite mark burns with sudden intensity, a searing pain that claws at my skin, demanding to be scratched, to be torn open. The memory is too vivid, too painful, and panic wells up inside me, choking off my breath. My body writhes in Vaughn's arms as I fight the urge to claw at the burning mark on my shoulder, to rip it out of my flesh and rid myself of the torment that it brings.

To rid myself of Adam forever.

Desperation claws at my chest as I bury my nose in the crook of his neck, inhaling deeply, trying to drown out the memory with the comfort of Vaughn's bittersweet scent. My tongue flicks out again, lapping at his pulse point, drawing a groan of pleasure from his lips. I claw at his chest, my nails scraping against his skin as I press closer. I'm consumed by my instincts. All I can think about is drowning in him, letting him consume me until there's nothing left but the searing pleasure of his touch.

I'm settled onto a bed of blankets and shirts, the familiar scents of my pack mingling together, surrounding me like a cocoon. The soft fabric drapes over me, forming a makeshift nest that's supposed to bring comfort. But instead of soothing my instincts, the sensation is suffocating. Everything feels like it's pressing in on me, the walls of the nest closing in, amplifying the panic in my chest. My breathing becomes ragged, my heart pounding in my ears as I glance up at Creed, then back at Vaughn.

My core throbs, and my mouth waters. The sight of Vaughn—shirtless, his broad shoulders and sculpted chest glistening slightly in the low light—drives me to the edge. His skin is already marked by my nails and teeth, my claim on him visible. He's wearing low-slung basketball shorts that hang on his hips, a towel clutched in his left hand. His nostrils flare as he scents me, and I can see the struggle in his eyes, the way his control wavers as he fights against the pull of my heat.

"You want me, Vaughn," I whisper. "You know you do. Stop fighting it."

He tenses, his breath hitching as he fights against his own instincts. "Doll," he warns, his voice thick with concern. "You're not yourself right now. This heat—it's making you do things you wouldn't normally do. I don't want to take advantage of you." But his words do little to quell the frantic need surging through me. My body acts on its own accord, driven by the need to taste him fully.

I slide down to the floor at his feet and my gaze travels up his chiseled chest which is dripping in ink, an intricate serpent tattoo coiling up his torso.

"Kaylani," Vaughn rasps, but there's a tremor in his voice that betrays his own loss of control. He's on the edge, just like me, and it only makes me want him more. He looks like a dark god—sharp angles and black orbs I could get lost in. I want to worship at his altar. The slick between my thighs increases as I reach up, tugging at the waistband of his shorts, desperate to taste him, to feel him.

"This is my fucking choice," I growl as he hesitates, his muscles tensing, but the look in his eyes tells me he's not going to stop me. A shiver of satisfaction rolls through me like molten lava. For once, I'm in control, and I'm going to revel in it.

I pull his shorts down just enough to free him, his thick, heavy cock springing free. My mouth waters even more, the sight of him making me ache with need. Without waiting for permission, I lean in, pressing my lips to the tip of his cock. The salty tang of his pre-cum bursts on my tongue and we both groan in unison. With the flat of my tongue I lick him from base to tip, swirling my tongue around the head before sucking him deep into the back of my throat. The taste of him floods my senses—a rich, dark bitterness like the finest chocolate. It's an addictive flavor, one that I can't get enough of, and it drives me to take him deeper, to savor every inch of his length as I slide my lips down his shaft. I'm dizzy with need, each stroke of my tongue against him sending sparks of pleasure through my body.

I want more.

My hands land on his thighs as I adjust my position at his feet, taking him in my mouth deeper, faster. Hollowing my lips and sucking as much of his delicious taste into my mouth as I can. Vaughn hisses and the sound sends a shock of pleasure shooting like lightning straight to my core. I swallow his length deeper, taking him as far as I can. His cock hits the back of my throat forcing me to gag around his shaft.

"*Yesss* just like that," he moans as the muscles in my throat squeeze him tighter. His praise spurs me on. I force my throat to relax and his cock fills my mouth completely, his girth stretching my jaw to the point it's aching. But I welcome the pain, letting it fuel the frenzy building inside me.

"Fuck, doll," Vaughn curses as his hand comes to rest on the back of my head, his fingers tangling in my hair as I take him deeper into my mouth. His hips jerk involuntarily, pushing him further into my throat, and his hands in my hair force me to stay where I am, holding him deep in the back of my throat.

Creed's voice filters through the haze of my need, a distant murmur that barely registers as I surrender to Vaughn's pleasure. His cock stretches my lips wide as I take him deep, his thick fingers gripping my hair roughly. With each thrust he slides in and out of my throat. My eyes water. The burn in my throat is searing, choking me as I try to swallow him down.

It's overwhelming.

I can barely breathe, each thrust becoming more frantic as he growls and curses under his breath. I'm enveloped by his scent, his taste, and the sinful sounds he makes.

I can't stop, wouldn't even if I could.

The desperate need to have him fill my mouth with his release, to drain his pleasure.

I'm feral for it.

Vaughn's cock twitches in my throat, growing harder with each passing second. I cling to the fabric around his hips, my grip so tight my fingers ache as I bob my head, frantic to take all of him and quell the ravenous hunger inside me. His grip tightens in my hair, and I can sense the moment he's about to lose control. I think he's going to let me push him over the edge, but then he pulls back abruptly, his cock slipping free from my mouth with a wet pop. A trail of saliva connects us briefly before snapping away, severing the connection. I whimper at the sudden loss, tears of frustration welling in my eyes as I look up at him, my body trembling with desperation. Panting, I fall to one hip, staring up at his face, which is twisted with guilt and conflict.

"Why the fuck wouldn't you finish?" I demand, struggling to my feet. My body shakes under the strain, every muscle vibrating with the intensity of my need. I collapse on the edge of the bed as I wait for him to respond.

Vaughn doesn't answer me, making disappointment and frustration roll through me in equal measure. He looks at Creed, his own frustration evident in the way he clenches his jaw. With a growl of exasperation, he tucks his cock back into his shorts, his hand rubbing wearily down his face.

"I'm going to get you some water. I'll be right back," Creed murmurs, his voice gentle as he leans down to press a kiss to my forehead. The warmth of his lips lingers for a brief moment before he pulls away.

I watch the strong muscles of his back flex as he disappears through the door, leaving me and Vaughn alone. His dark onyx eyes caress my curves, my nipples pebbling under the intensity. It's like a physical weight that makes my heat spike for him. My core throbs again. Desperate and aching to be filled. My fingers trail down my body and into my slick, fingers drumming along my clit. But the sensation does little to stem the ache building.

"You didn't have to stop," I say, my fingers swirling around my clit. "It was my choice, Vaughn." I spread my thighs further. "I wanted to taste you. To get you off." I push two fingers deep inside me and Vaughn growls as he watches me, but he doesn't move closer to the bed as my fingers dive into my pussy deeper, gathering my arousal and dragging my fingers back to my clit. I moan and Vaughn's body tenses.

"Fuck me," I demand, my voice breathless and full of urgency.

"Doll," Vaughn warns, his voice strained with the effort of holding back. "It's hard enough not to give in to your pheromones without you begging too, sweetheart. But I can't take advantage of you like this." His words are forced, each one sounding like it's being dragged from him as he struggles to maintain control. "I won't do it."

The rejection sends a surge of irritation through me, my heat-fueled instincts pushing me to the edge of reason. "Coward," I taunt, my voice laced with frustration and desire. I pull my fingers from my dripping cunt and swipe them over my nipples, feeling the slickness transfer to my hardened peaks. I pluck and pull at them, the sensation sending jolts of pleasure through me, but it's not enough. I need more. I need him. Spreading my legs wider, I give him an unobstructed view of my arousal, my body on full display for him.

I should be embarrassed—humiliated even. I've never been this crass, this bold. But the heat is driving me to the brink, making me do things I wouldn't normally do. Maybe Vaughn's right. Maybe I'm not in my right mind.

But I don't care. I want him now.

The need is overwhelming, consuming every rational thought, leaving only the burning desire to be filled by him, to have him claim me in the most primal way. My breath comes in shallow bursts, my chest heaving with the intensity of my longing as I continue to tease and torment myself, hoping to break through his resolve.

"Vaughn," I breathe, my voice a desperate plea. "Please..."

But he stays rooted in place, his body trembling with restraint. The internal battle is clear in his eyes, the conflict between his need to protect me and his desire to give in to what we both want. It's a thin line he's walking, and I can see it fraying with every passing second. The tension in the room is suffocating, thick with need, and I can feel my own control slipping further away. My body is on fire, every nerve ending screaming for release, and the sight of Vaughn standing there, holding back, only makes it worse.

I need him. Now.

Vaughn's gaze darkens, his eyes narrowing as he steps forward, the tension in his body radiating off him in waves. He moves closer, his presence overwhelming as he towers over me and the heat between us intensifies, a fire that threatens to consume us both. For a moment, he hovers over me, his breath scorching against my skin. I can feel the war raging within him—the struggle between his instincts and his desire to protect me. But as I meet his gaze, the raw hunger in his eyes mirrors my own, and I sense he's on the brink of breaking. So I push him over the edge.

"I'm choosing this Vaughn," I say. "I'm choosing *you*."

His resolve crumbles in an instant. "God damn it," he curses, his voice low and strained as his hand shoots out. He grabs my wrist, yanking my fingers from my aching core and bringing them to his lips. His tongue flicks out, tasting the slick on my fingers, a low growl vibrating through him as he savors the essence of me.

"You're so damn infuriating," he murmurs, his voice dark and dangerous, sending a shiver down my spine. "I should punish you for teasing me."

I moan at the sound of his dark threat, a thrill running through me at the thought of his punishment. "*YESSS*," I hiss, stretching out the word. "Take me. Use me. Punish me."

Vaughn's control snaps. In a blur of movement, he's on me, his mouth crashing down on mine in a bruising kiss—teeth and tongue clashing with desperate need. His body presses me into the soft nest of blankets, his hands roaming my body with rough, demanding touches that ignite sparks of pleasure wherever they land.

His lips trail down my neck, biting and sucking at my sensitive skin, leaving a scorching trail of fire in their wake. My fingers dig into his broad shoulders, desperate to pull him closer as the ache inside me swells to an unbearable level. The intensity of our connection flips a switch within me, igniting a frenzy of need and desire.

"Vaughn..." I gasp, my back arching off the bed as his hand finds my soaked core. His fingers slide through my slick folds, three fingers pushing into my pussy with a deep, delicious stretch that makes me cry out. "Ahhh!"

His mouth claims mine again, silencing my cries of pleasure as his fingers thrust into me—harder, faster—filling me with a relentless rhythm that has me teetering on the edge of release in seconds.

But it's still not enough.

"More," I demand, my hips bucking against his hand as I seek a deeper, more intense touch. I need a knot. My inner voice taunts, but my alpha isn't here.

Vaughn pulls his dripping fingers free and presses them against my lips, forcing me to taste myself. "You said you wanted to taste me, doll? Be a good girl and suck my fingers clean while I fuck you."

With his free hand, he positions himself between my thighs, the head of his cock pressing teasingly against my entrance, promising the release I so desperately crave. I can feel the tension in his body, his barely restrained need as he holds himself back, waiting for my submission. I obey, taking his fingers deep into my mouth, savoring the taste of myself. We both groan in unison, the sound raw and filled with need.

"That's it, doll. Let me use you however I see fit." With a low, feral growl, Vaughn thrusts into me, his cock stretching and filling me in a way that makes stars explode behind my eyes. The sensation is overwhelming, the pleasure bordering on pain, but I revel in it, needing every inch of him to quell the raging fire inside me.

He doesn't hold back, his movements fierce and possessive as he claims me with every thrust. His free hand grips my hips, pulling me against him with a bruising force, each thrust sending waves of pleasure crashing through me. My moans are muffled around his fingers, my eyes rolling back as I surrender to the intoxicating blend of pleasure and pain produced under his dominating touch.

I cling to him, my nails digging into his shoulders as I ride the wave of sensation, my body trembling with the force of my release. He pulls his fingers from my mouth with a loud pop, his wet fingers pressing against my throat as I scream through another orgasm, a tidal wave of pleasure consuming me and forcing my vision to narrow to a tunnel of bliss.

CHAPTER 12
Creed

A S I MAKE MY way to the kitchen upstairs to grab Kay some water, I chuckle to myself, imagining just how hard Vaughn is trying to resist Kay. I don't think he needs to worry about taking advantage of her. She was pretty clear on what she wanted. Hopefully the alone time will get him out of his head.

I'm stopped in my tracks at the door frame into the loft when I notice Hux sitting on the couch, his head bent low, hands covering his face. Guilt settles heavy in my chest at the sight. I snapped at him earlier, telling him to leave the room was for Kay's sake, but seeing him like this now, I know it's tearing him apart. His need to protect her, to be by her side, is as strong as mine, and pushing him away is probably driving him crazy.

My poor alpha.

"Hux?" I call softly.

His body stiffens, and he slowly glances up at me. The wild look in his eyes makes my gut clench. Frantic and searching, his nostrils flare as he scents the air, desperately seeking Kay's scent. My skin is saturated with her rose perfume, and I know his instincts are screaming that she's nearby.

"Creed," he croaks, getting to his feet with a quick, almost jerky movement. "What's wrong? Is Kay okay? What happened?"

The questions come rapid-fire, his voice laced with anxiety. I hold up a hand to placate him, trying to keep my own composure in check. But deep down, I don't know if she's okay. I wasn't when it happened to me, and memories of how out of control I felt resurface.

But I will do anything I can to help her through this.

"She's fine, alpha," I soothe, making sure to keep my tone steady. "She's in my nest with Vaughn. I just came upstairs to get her some water."

His shoulders sag in relief, but the tension in his body doesn't fully ease. "Good." He mutters the word, but his gaze drifts away from mine, landing on the floor. The spicy scent of his anxiety hangs in the air, thick and heavy, practically tangible.

I hesitate for a moment, watching him as he tries to compose himself. It's clear that he's struggling, torn between wanting to be near Kay and respecting the boundaries I've set. I know how much she means to him, how much he's sacrificing to keep her safe. Because I care about her just as much.

If it were me, I'd be going insane too.

"Why don't you go into your office. Into your viewing room?" I suggest, hoping to offer him some semblance of comfort.

This wouldn't be the first time Hux used that one-way mirror to watch. He doesn't think I know, but Candi caught him watching during one of my heats.

He's a secret voyeur.

His brows shoot up in surprise, the first real sign of hope I've seen from him since I walked in. "You'd be okay with me watching you with her?" he asks, his voice tinged with uncertainty.

I chuckle, stepping fully into the room. "This wouldn't be the first time you've watched me and Vaughn."

A heavy silence descends as he realizes I've known all along that he likes to watch me. He swallows thickly, and my smirk widens as I head toward the kitchen, pulling open the fridge to grab a bottle of water before turning to face him again. "You should be there, Hux. She's our omega, and she needs her alpha near. Mine and Vaughn's scents may not hurt her, but she needs you." I pause, letting the words sink in. "I need you there too."

"You do?" he croaks.

"Yes." I let the word hang in the air for a moment, watching as he absorbs what I'm saying. "I think she would be more comfortable knowing you were close by. She misses you. When she was asleep in the bathtub, she called out for you."

"She did?" he asks, his voice thick with emotion.

I nod, taking a step closer. "Yeah, she did. She needs you, Hux. We all do. You're our alpha."

The weight of my words settles over him, and I watch as the tension in his body slowly melts away. His shoulders slump, and the strained look in his eyes softens.

"I knew that Michelle wanted to break her and Adam's bond, Creed. That she planned to kill her. I knew, and I didn't tell her," Hux confesses, his voice heavy with regret.

I run a hand through my disheveled hair, a sigh escaping my lips. "I know. And you kept it from me, too, Hux."

He drags a hand over his peppered beard, his blue eyes locking with mine. "I'm sorry. It was hard being trapped down there. The only thing keeping me going was the fact that I was going to be bringing my kitten's best friend home. And I failed her."

The raw vulnerability in his voice hits me hard, and his scent carries a bitter tang of regret and self-reproach. It's a side of him I've rarely seen—stripped of the alpha's usual control and strength.

My heart aches at the sight of his brokenness. My omega instincts surge, urging me to offer comfort. I step forward, wrapping my arms around him in a tight embrace.

Hux tenses for a moment before his arms come around me, pulling me close. The warmth of his body against mine is a grounding presence, and I can feel his breath shuddering as he tries to hold back his emotions.

"I should have been there for her," he murmurs into my shoulder, his voice muffled by the fabric of my shirt.

"My mother is to blame for this, Hux," I whisper, gently rubbing his back. "She is the one who accused you of killing Dane. She forced all those omegas to take Heat, including me. None of that is your fault."

He nods, his grip on me tightening. "But I should have at least protected her from Adam."

I lean back to look him in the eyes. "Be there for her now. She needs our alpha during her heat, Hux. She's confused and in pain. As an omega, the only ones who can help her through that are her pack. And that includes you."

"But I can't be in the same room as her without hurting her more."

"Go to the viewing room. Comfort her from a distance."

We stand there for a few moments, offering each other silent comfort. The tension between us eases as we both take solace in this shared understanding of our roles and responsibilities.

CHAPTER 13
Kaylani

A S THE AFTERSHOCKS OF another climax ripple through me, a cry of pleasure escapes my lips. Vaughn's grip on my throat releases and he smooths back my hair from my sweaty face, murmuring sweet praise into my ear. His look of complete adoration steals whatever breath I have left in my lungs. There's something about being in Vaughn's arms like this. He makes me feel safe, protected, and dare I say it... loved too. My eyes prick with tears, emotions spiraling out of control. The warmth of his body against mine is a comfort I've only ever found with him, and in these moments the world outside fades away.

"What is it, doll? What's on your mind?" Vaughn's voice is soft, his dark eyes searching mine with a tenderness that pulls me in. It's the same look he gives Creed. "You know you can tell me anything, right?"

The warmth in his voice tightens my chest. I force a watery smile, trying to hold myself together. His presence is calming, and I don't want to ruin this moment with the storm raging inside me. One hand braces himself above me while the other smooths a stray strand of hair from my face. That simple gesture makes my heart ache with longing.

"I've been thinking a lot," I start, my voice wavering slightly. "About everything... about *Adam*." His name tastes bitter on my tongue, but I need to say it. I need to face it.

Vaughn's eyes darken, his grip on me tightening just a fraction. "You don't have to talk about him if you're not ready," he murmurs, but I shake my head.

"No, I need to," I insist, my voice growing stronger. "I told Liam I wanted to take Adam down. Make him pay for everything he has done to me. To my pack." I exhale heavily. "It's the only way I'll ever be free of him, of the nightmares. But to do that, I need to learn how to defend myself."

His brows knit together in concern, but there's also a spark of understanding in his eyes. "Kay, you don't have to do this alone. We're all here to protect you."

"I know," I whisper, my heart swelling at the thought of my pack standing behind me. "But this is something I have to do for myself. I need to be able to fight back. I need to know that if I ever face him again, I won't be helpless. I won't be that scared girl he tried to break."

The memories of those dark times flash in my mind—Vaughn holding me as I trembled in Hux's bed all those months ago. Of him chasing away my nightmares after the night at the estate when he saved me from Adam. I've always felt safe with Vaughn, and I know he would have killed Adam that night if I'd let him. In fact, for a moment I had thought he did. But I need to be able to stand on my own two feet.

I can't rely on my pack for this. I need to take back some control in my life. Fight back. For once. For me. I meet Vaughn's gaze again as he patiently waits for me to continue. He really is the perfect beta.

"I want you to teach me to fight," I say, my voice firm. "You're the only one I trust to show me how to defend myself."

Vaughn's eyes widen in surprise, but there's a flicker of pride in them too. He studies me for a long moment, as if weighing my resolve. "You're serious about this."

"I've never been more serious about anything," I reply, holding his gaze. "I need to do this, Vaughn. I need to be strong enough to face Adam, to take back control of my life. I hid behind Heat in fear of what would happen when my heat actually came. I was afraid I would let Adam in again, afraid he would hurt me. I don't want to feel that helpless ever again."

He exhales slowly, his hand cupping my cheek with a gentleness that makes my chest tighten. "Alright, doll. I'll teach you. But know this—you're already stronger than you think. You've survived things most people wouldn't even be able to comprehend. But if learning to fight brings you some semblance of control, I would be honored to teach you."

Relief washes over me, and I lean into his touch, closing my eyes. "Thank you. I couldn't do this without you."

"You're mine to protect. Remember? Always," he promises. "I'll help you face your fears on your terms, and you'll finally be free." His words sink into me, giving me the strength I need to keep going. Vaughn, believing in me, believing I can fight back and take control of my life again, begins to settle the storm raging inside me. It's like a lifeline, anchoring me to the possibility of a future where I'm not defined by my past, but by the strength I've found to overcome it.

Just then, a deep voice groans from the doorway.

"Damn, seeing the two of you together is so fucking sexy." Creed stands there holding a bottle of water, his chest heaving with every breath. His eyes flicker between Vaughn and me, a raw hunger in his gaze.

"Creed," I moan unabashedly, the sight of him only intensifying the need coursing through me.

Vaughn pulls back, his breath coming in ragged pants as he glances over at Creed. The slight shift of his hips drags out a moan of pleasure from me, each movement intensifying the ache inside. My heart races. If I can't have my alpha's knot, I'll have both my omega and beta together.

"About fucking time you got here, love. Our little minx is insatiable and needs a knot." Vaughn's dark gaze shifts back to me, filled with dark promises that make me shiver in anticipation of what's to come. "So we'll have to improvise."

Creed pads across the room to the side of the bed, his caramel scent enveloping me. My body reacts to him, instantly clamping down on Vaughn's cock. "Fuck," he groans, his head falling back in pleasure as my pussy pulses.

"Give her some water before I lose my fucking mind," Vaughn commands, his voice tight with restraint.

Creed doesn't hesitate, gently lifting my head and helping me drink the cool liquid. I gulp it down greedily, some of it spilling past my lips and pooling on the nest of blankets beneath me. When Vaughn slips free, stepping back from the bed, I can't help the moan of protest that escapes my lips.

"What are you doing?" I ask, my body trembling with unspent need.

Vaughn palms his still-hard cock, a wicked smirk playing on his lips. "Like I said, doll. Creed and I don't have a knot. But there are other ways to keep you satisfied."

Creed wipes my forehead with a damp cloth, his touch soothing as he sets the half-empty water bottle on the side table. Despite his gentle care, my gaze is locked on Vaughn, my heart racing with anticipation.

"If you need to rest, tiny, just say the word, okay?" Creed's eyes meet mine, and sensing my hesitation, he adds, "You're in control of all this. You know that, don't you?" His hand settles on my hip, a steadying presence in the midst of my chaos.

"I want you both," I breathe out, my voice shaky with desire.

"Then get up, Kaylani," Creed growls, sending a shiver down my spine. Slowly, I rise on unsteady legs, Creed supporting my elbow as he steers me toward the floor to ceiling mirror.

"Look at that slick pouring down your legs," Creed moans into my ear, his teeth grazing my skin with a soft nip. I suck in a sharp breath, my nerves tingling with anticipation. The uncertainty of when another wave of pain might strike only heightens my tension.

"Now, tiny, you have a decision to make," Creed whispers, his breath hot against my ear. My gaze flicks to Vaughn, searching for answers.

"Is he there?" Vaughn asks, his smile widening as he glances at the mirror.

I furrow my brows in confusion. "What are you talking about?" I ask, turning my gaze to Creed.

"This is a one-way glass," Creed explains, his voice laced with dark promises. "You might have an admirer, tiny. Do you want to be watched?"

My heart races at the thought of someone on the other side of the glass, but the only one I want watching is Hux. If he can't be in the room with us, at least he's close. Knowing that he's watching sends another wave of slick down my thighs. I press my legs together, trying to contain the surge of arousal, but Vaughn steps up behind me, chuckling wickedly into my ear and making my thighs even wetter.

"I think she likes the idea of him watching," Creed teases, though there's an undercurrent of anticipation in his voice.

Vaughn's chest brushes against my back, trapping me between them once more in this swirling vortex of sensation. Creed's teasing only fuels my desire, making me want them even more.

"Decide, doll," Vaughn taunts, his lips trailing kisses along my jaw. His large hand wraps around the back of my neck, gently squeezing as Creed's hand rests on the front of my throat, their fingertips touching, completely trapping me at their mercy.

"I want Hux to watch," I murmur, going in their arms.

Vaughn scoops me up, nestling me into his chest. "That's a good girl, good choice," he chuckles, carrying me back to Creed's nest.

Creed's nest.

The thought reminds me I don't have one of my own and my gaze flicks back to the wall of mirrors. I stare back at my disheveled self, pink hair plastered to my forehead, cheeks flushed. Mascara runs down my face, and I look terrible, but there's a wideness in my eyes I've never seen before, and right now, I don't care what I look like. The girl staring back at me isn't afraid, isn't nervous, and it's invigorating. Any doubt or uncertainty I had just been feeling evaporates instantly and I feel freed.

"So, is Hux really on the other side of the mirror?" I ask as Vaughn gently places me back on the nest of blankets, coating me in my pack scent.

Fresh brewed coffee.

The bed dips as Creed crawls up next to me, his mouth finding my neck again as he sucks on my pulse point.

"Does that turn you on, doll? Knowing our alpha is about to watch us both fuck you at the same time?" Vaughn growls darkly.

I turn away from the girl in the mirror to find Vaughn standing there, his tattoos on full display, each one telling a story. A sheen of sweat coats his abs and he's never looked more delicious. "Yesss," I slur as I drink him in.

Creed's lips ghost against my skin as he murmurs, "I want you so bad, tiny." The desperation in my omega's voice sends shivers cascading down my body. I moan, closing my eyes as I savor his caramel scent and his soft lips against my heated skin.

"Pet, lay down on the bed like a good boy," Vaughn demands. My eyes crack open at the darkness and heat in his voice.

It drives me wild.

As Creed crawls up the bed, Vaughn's gaze follows him with a mix of longing and intensity that takes my breath away. The love in his eyes is undeniable, a dark and devious devotion that he tries to mask with his usual smirk.

But I see it, clear as day. Even through my own haze.

Once Creed is in position, Vaughn's eyes shift back to me, catching me in the act of watching him. My heart skips a beat as our eyes lock, and I quickly drop my gaze, following the curves of his chest down to the patch of hair that leads to where his hand is lazily pumping his cock. My mouth goes dry at the sight, the tension in the room thickening as desire courses through me.

I might have just had him but I wasn't done with my beta yet.

"Do you wanna be my little doll, Kaylani? Let me use you?" Vaughn asks, biting his lip.

The memory of when I first questioned him about calling me his doll flashes in my mind. He'd kissed me and said, *I call you my doll because of your strength, your beauty, and the light you bring to those around you.* Then, he kissed away my doubts. And now, with the heat surging through me, I want it. I want to be his little doll. Because now I trust him not to break me.

"Yes I do," I practically beg, the words spilling from my lips without hesitation.

"Good. Now crawl your sexy ass up the bed and show me how you can please *our* pet." Vaughn's gaze slides between Creed and me, a wicked smile exposing his perfectly white teeth. "He looks hot for you, doll. Seeing his beta and omega fucking has gotten him nice and hard for you. Now get up there and soothe the ache you've caused him." I do as he demands, my core throbbing in anticipation.

Creed and Vaughn exchange a charged look, a silent conversation I can't focus on. My hands land on Creed's chest, and my body shivers as I settle my slit over his raging hard-on

"FUUCCKKK," Creed groans as he pulls me down on top of him. We both gasp as I sink down, feeling him stretch me deliciously.

But it's not enough.

I need more.

I let out a whimper of frustration, yearning for the complete fullness only a knot can provide. "Don't you worry, we know what you want," Vaughn murmurs, his voice a low purr. "You want to be stuffed so full of cock you can't even move, can't even think."

He crawls up the edge of the bed behind me, brushing my hair off my shoulder and biting it softly. The sensation sends a shiver down my spine, my eyes falling closed. My body is a whirlwind of pleasure and frustration, craving more, needing that final piece to make everything complete. Vaughn's hands begin their descent down the curves of my back, settling on my hips. He lifts my hips and thrusts me back down on Creed's cock, making us both moan in pleasure as he controls our movements.

But still, it's not enough, and I let out another whimper.

Vaughn shushes me, his fingers trailing down the crack of my ass, settling at the junction between my thighs. His fingers push into my pussy alongside Creed's cock, and I gasp at the unexpected intrusion.

"What are you doing?" I ask, having been expecting him to enter through the back, not in the same hole as Creed. He pushes deeper, his fingers moving in rhythm with Creed's thrusts. After a few strokes, he adds another finger, spreading them wide inside me. Creed and I groan in unison and my pleasure builds higher until I'm teetering on the edge.

"That's it, my doll. Take it, take your pleasure like a good girl," Vaughn growls, pulling his fingers free. His sticky hand finds the middle of my back, and he presses me down until I'm flush against Creed's chest, panting for breath. I glance over my shoulder at him as Creed begins to toy with the strands of my hair, his breath warm against my face.

Am I really doing this?

Two dicks... in the same hole.

Oh god, how are they both going to fit?

My eyes flicker to the mirror again, knowing Hux is watching us from the other side. The thought of my alpha nearby settles the storm inside me to a dull roar, grounding me in the chaos.

"Relax, pet," Vaughn purrs in my ear, the sound of him calling me 'pet' sending a shiver of anticipation through my body. I loved seeing him dominate Creed, and knowing he's about to do the same to me makes my breath come in ragged gasps.

His hands grip my hips, lifting them just enough to position his cock alongside Creed's. Slowly, he lowers me onto them both, and I cry out, my hands clutching at the sheets as my body tenses from the overwhelming stretch.

"Relax, my beautiful, precious pet. That's an order," Vaughn growls through gritted teeth, trying to hold back from thrusting into me fully. "You're doing a good job, my little doll," he adds as the stretch of them both steals my breath.

"Wait!" I scream, a sudden wave of fear washing over me. Everything feels like it's spinning out of control, and the only thing I want is my alpha. "I want to see Hux," I whimper, my voice trembling.

I know the scent of an alpha could push me over the edge, but I hope that seeing Hux's steady, calm presence will help me through this. My body shakes as I hold myself in position, teetering on the edge of pleasure and panic, desperately clinging to the thought of my alpha to steady me.

I watch Creed's reflection as he nods toward the mirror, and suddenly, the glass reveals another room on the other side, furnished with two lounge chairs and a coffee table. Hux stands behind them, arms crossed over his broad chest, his tie loosened and hanging limp against his fitted shirt.

"Alpha?" I whisper, my voice trembling.

"It's okay, kitten. I'm right here," he says, his voice coming over a loud-speaker in the room. I let out a shaky breath just hearing his voice as it settles something inside of me. Creed continues to play with my hair, nestling his nose into me, marking me with his scent.

I let out a satisfied moan.

Without realizing it, my body has already begun to relax, and Vaughn slides another inch into me. With how wet I am, there is little resistance. A collective groan echoes from my pack, my alpha's loud and sexy over the speaker.

"That's it, tiny," Creed says, his voice a soothing balm as he continues to stroke my face with gentle touches. I look up into his bright green eyes, his brow coated in sweat, and find a strange sense of comfort in his intense gaze.

"On the count of three, pet," Vaughn warns, his voice thick with desire. His hands on my back move to my hips, spreading my cheeks and massaging them gently. "One," he begins, slowly pushing inside me, and I groan alongside Creed.

"Two. Almost there, pet. You look so fucking hot stuffed full of our cocks," Vaughn chuckles darkly, his tone sending shivers down my spine.

"What are you doing just--" I cry out as he bottoms out inside of me, pulling my hips towards him. The most delicious pain and pleasure I've ever experienced in my life cascades through my body in waves, my eyes rolling to the back of my head as I try to catch my breath. Creed's massive hands pull me closer, pushing me up and down both of their shafts. I can think of nothing else, feel nothing else but them. I'm surrounded by their scents, their sounds, the wet symphony of my slick echoing around the room.

"You look beautiful, kitten," Hux's voice rumbles over the speaker, deep and commanding. "Eyes on me when you come." The alpha bark in his tone is impossible to resist, a primal command that sends a thrill through me.

I force my eyes open and lock onto him in the mirror. His sleeves are rolled up to his elbows, his tie discarded on the coffee table, and his cock is gripped tightly in his right hand. The other hand is pressed against the mirror, as if he's trying to reach through the glass to me. He looks like a tattooed god, every inch of him taut and powerful as he watches us, pumping in rhythm with Vaughn's movements.

Pleasure crashes over me, twisting my stomach into delicious, painful knots that steal my breath.

"FUCK!" Creed yells, his hands digging into my back as he comes deep inside me. The intensity of our shared release leaves us both limp, collapsing into each other as the pleasure begins to fade.

But Vaughn doesn't stop.

He lifts me as if I weigh nothing, slamming me back down again and again until he too groans, his release filling me alongside Creed's. "Damn, my filthy little pets," he pants. I glance over my shoulder at him, too spent to form a proper response. A satisfied smirk paints his lips as we all collapse onto the nest of blankets, their cocks still buried deep inside me. Vaughn slaps my ass—hard—and I let out a breathy moan, too satisfied to care. Too content to just be within their arms.

Chapter 14

Hux

My mind replays the events in slow motion, the images refusing to fade no matter how hard I try to shake them away. Kay's fear-stricken eyes, wide and pleading, her pained cries that seemed to rip through the silence like a blade—every moment echoes in my head, an endless loop of torment that tightens its grip on my sanity. I clutch the bathroom sink so hard my knuckles turn white, the cold porcelain grounding me even as a growl of frustration rumbles in my chest, threatening to break free like a caged beast.

Three fucking days.

Three excruciatingly long days of watching her suffer, watching her pleasure at a distance. I kept my distance, but all I wanted was to be there for her, to hold her, to whisper in her ear that everything would be okay. But I couldn't.

The mere thought of her taking Heat, of the destruction it could bring, claws at my mind, relentless and unforgiving. The images of her writhing in pain, trembling uncontrollably, her body betraying her—Kay could have died. That possibility seizes me with a cold terror that sinks deep into my bones, a fear I can't shake no matter how much I try.

If I hadn't been so damn focused on hiding Michelle's plans, maybe I would have seen the signs sooner. Maybe I could have stopped this from happening. But I thought I was protecting her. I thought keeping her at the Den would keep her safe, shield her from the darkness closing in around us. It was a stupid fantasy, a delusion that I could control the uncontrollable.

It's only a matter of time before Michelle demands that all of Sterling's unmated omegas register with the Bramwell Sanctuary, and that's a problem we aren't ready to face. Not yet. Candi, Creed, Kay—three omegas in my care, three lives that depend on me. I can't afford to fail them, but the weight of that responsibility is crushing me.

Pixie installed new cameras yesterday, and for a brief moment, they eased the gnawing anxiety in my chest. But I know it's not enough. It's never enough. The paperwork on my desk is piling up, overflowing with the responsibilities of reopening the Den to the public. Everything is spiraling out of control, but none of it matters right now.

All I care about is Kay.

I lift my gaze to the mirror, barely recognizing the man staring back at me. The face is worn, lined with the stress of too many sleepless nights, my beard is more gray than black these days. Dark circles shadow my eyes, making me look older, more exhausted. I sigh, turning on the faucet and splashing cold water on my face, but it does nothing to cool the fire raging inside me. My cock has been hard for hours, throbbing with a need that only she can satisfy. The idea of anyone else easing her heat is unbearable.

I'm supposed to be her alpha, her protector, yet I've been reduced to a bystander, helpless as she suffers.

My reflection stares back at me, a man changed by the past few months—eyes harder, darker, filled with a desperation I can barely contain. "I should have been in there with her," I murmur to myself, my voice a harsh rasp in the empty bathroom.

My responsibilities as an alpha go beyond just protecting. I'm supposed to nurture, provide, and ensure the safety of my pack. I've failed them in so many ways, and the thought alone is enough to drive me to my knees.

Creed and Vaughns broken bond.

Adam hurting Kay.

Kay getting hooked on Heat.

Candice, my sister, dealing with my absence.

All the things I missed, the things that I didn't protect my pack from, weigh down on me. But I can't afford to be paralyzed by it. I have to push forward, to be better, stronger. For Kay, for our pack. I'll become whatever I need to be to keep them safe.

The passage of time has done little to ease the tension coiled tight within me. It's getting harder and harder to keep my distance. The memory of her pain is still fresh, a wound that refuses to heal. And the more time passes, the more I realize how much I need her.

I can't stay away any longer.

With renewed determination, I leave the bathroom and head towards Creed's nest, my heart pounding with a mix of fear and hope. I need to see her, to make sure she's okay. The thought of her alone, suffering, tears at me.

"Kitten, can I come in?" I call softly as I push open the door. My pack's pheromones hit me like a freight train, and I greedily inhale their scents, grounding myself in the familiar mix of comfort and desire. Vaughn and Creed are tangled together fast asleep in the nest. Alone.

Kay isn't here.

A cold knot of panic tightens in my chest as I scan the empty space.

Where is she?

I race through the bottom floor of the club, each empty room only heightening my anxiety. My heart pounds in my ears, the silence mocking me with every step.

Fuck.

I take the stairs two at a time, my mind racing as fast as my feet. The upstairs loft looms before me, and I head straight for my room, clinging to the desperate hope that Candi was right—that Kay has been spending every night in my bed, finding some solace there. I push open the door, expecting to see her curled up in the sheets, but the room is empty. Her scent lingers, wrapping around me like a cruel reminder, but it offers no comfort, only a deepening sense of dread. My eyes dart to the bed, where the blanket is conspicuously missing. My heart skips a beat, the dread turning into a full-blown panic.

Where the hell is she?

Don't panic.

Every dark thought rushes to the surface, threatening to overwhelm me—Adam finding her, the Hounds taking her from me. A million and one scenarios whirl through my mind, each more terrifying than the last. But no, the alarms would have gone off. We would have known.

I fumble in my pocket for my phone, pulling up the camera feed with trembling fingers. But there's nothing—no movement notifications, no alerts, nothing to suggest anyone has breached the Den. Yet the gnawing anxiety refuses to relent. I need to see for myself. My breath comes in shallow bursts as I flip through each camera feed, scanning every corner of the Den.

The back alley. The bar. The hall outside my office. The stairs leading to the loft. All empty. I growl in frustration, feeling the walls closing in on me. Where else could she be? Just as I'm about to abandon the room and continue the search, a soft cry reaches my ears. It's so faint, I almost miss it—a sound muffled by the thick walls, but unmistakably coming from the direction of the closet. My heart clenches painfully in my chest as I approach, every instinct screaming at me to be prepared for the worst.

Why would she be in the closet?

I hesitate for a fraction of a second, my hand hovering over the doorknob. The fear of what I might find on the other side nearly paralyzes me, but I force myself to push the door open, bracing for whatever awaits me inside.

"Kay?" I call out, my voice trembling slightly as I push the door open. The sight that greets me makes my heart plummet. Kay is curled up in the back of my closet, clutching Vaughn's shirt to her chest like it's the only thing tethering her to this world. The sight breaks something deep inside me. Her distress is palpable, her rose scent tinged with something bitter and sour. Fear and despair interwoven with the sweetness. She deserves better than this—better than the cold, hard floor of a closet, surrounded by old clothes and blankets, seeking comfort in the darkness.

"Why are you on the floor, baby?" I ask softly, sliding down the wall next to her. The urge to pull her into my arms, to shelter her from whatever demons are chasing her, is almost overwhelming. But I hold back, not wanting to invade her space when she's clearly struggling.

Her body shakes with the force of her sobs, and she buries her face deeper into Vaughn's shirt, as if trying to disappear into the fabric. The sound of her crying cuts through me like a knife, and I'm torn between giving her the comfort she desperately needs and respecting her need to be alone. But when she finally looks up at me, her stormy gray eyes puffy and red, it shatters the last of my restraint.

"I feel so lost without her, Hux," she sobs, her voice cracking with the weight of her grief. "I thought she was dead this whole time. I had given up on her. If I had just tried harder..."

Her words trail off into another sob, and I can see the anguish etched into every line of her face. The pain she's carrying, the guilt she's shouldering—it's too much for anyone to bear. I can't stand to see her like this, so broken and lost.

I reach out and grab her, pulling her into my arms before I can second-guess myself. She collapses against me, her body trembling as I hold her close, my chest tightening as her bitter scent coats my tongue, masking the sweetness of her roses. A deep purr rumbles in my chest, a desperate attempt to soothe her pain, to comfort her in any way I can.

"Rebecca's death isn't your fault, kitten. It's mine," I admit softly, my voice barely above a whisper.

She looks up at me, her eyes wide with shock, silent tears tracking down her cheeks. I wipe them away with my thumbs, lifting her chin so she has to look at me. "It's not your fault," she whispers, her voice trembling. "You couldn't have known."

" I should have protected you both better," I say, my voice breaking with the weight of the confession. "I told her not to fight, Kay. She trusted me, and look where it got us. If I hadn't—"

She cuts me off, pressing her forehead against mine, grounding me in the warmth of her touch. "You did what you thought was best. You were trying to keep her safe. We've all made choices we regret, Hux. Her death isn't your fault, okay?" She leans back to look at me, her eyes pleading with me to believe her. "I don't blame you."

Her words are meant to soothe, but the guilt still gnaws at me, sharp and unforgiving. As her alpha I'm supposed to be the one soothing her. "I should have been stronger," I whisper, the confession slipping out before I can stop it. "For you. For Rebecca... For everyone."

She shakes her head, her fingers gripping Vaughn's shirt tighter as if drawing strength from it. "You've been strong, Hux. Stronger than any of us. But you can't carry all this alone. You can't keep things from us anymore."

I hold her tighter, my heart aching with the truth of her words. She's right. I've been carrying the weight of this for too long, trying to protect everyone, trying to be the alpha they need. But I'm only one man, and the burden is too heavy. "I just want to protect you. To make sure you're safe. And be the alpha you deserve... If you'll let me."

She looks up at me, her eyes softening, and for a moment, the fear and pain in them recede, replaced by something warm and hopeful. "I'm not going anywhere, Hux. I trust you." Her words, simple as they are, fill me with a resolve I didn't know I had left. I press a kiss to her forehead, my heart pounding as I vow to keep her safe.

No matter what it takes.

Her eyes drop to my lips briefly, and I growl softly at the thought of tasting her after all this time. The longing I've kept buried surges to the surface, making my pulse quicken. Our gazes lock, and I can see the same need mirrored in her eyes.

Slowly, she leans in, her breath mingling with mine.

My heart pounds in my chest, the world narrowing down to just the two of us. When her lips finally touch mine, it's like a dam breaking. The kiss is gentle at first, a tentative exploration, but the pent-up desire, the longing, and the grief soon take over. I deepen the kiss, pouring all my emotions into it, hoping she can feel how much I've missed her, how much I need her. A deep rumbling purr vibrates through me and her hands slide up to my neck, fingers tangling in my hair as she presses herself closer. The taste of her, the feel of her lips moving against mine, is intoxicating.

I pull back just enough to rest my forehead against hers, our breaths mingling in the small space between us. Her scent is stronger now, and I can physically feel another wave of heat coming on. The familiar mix of roses and something uniquely her fills my senses, making it hard to think clearly.

"Your heat is coming back kitten," I whisper, my voice heavy with concern. I know I should leave, get Vaughn and Creed. She needs them to get through this. All I do when I'm near her is hurt her.

But the thought of leaving her...

It twists something deep inside me, a primal instinct to stay and protect her, to be the one who comforts her. But I also know my presence could complicate things. I've always wanted to be the alpha she needs, but what if my being here does more harm than good?

"I know," she whispers, her voice trembling as her eyes gloss over with a fresh wave of tears. "It's why I came in here. I can't take another wave, Hux. I can't."

Her voice cracks, filled with desperation, and my frown deepens as I search her eyes, trying to understand. My gaze follows hers to a small white bottle lying on the floor, and my stomach drops.

She was going to take another Heat pill?

The realization hits me like a punch to the gut, and I clench my jaw tightly, trying to suppress the growl rising in my throat. The urge to bark out a command, to demand she never do something like that again, is almost overpowering. But I force myself to stop. I can't give in to my instinct to control or command her. Right now, I need to put her needs first—her fears, her mistakes. I need to be the alpha she can lean on, not the one who adds to her burden.

Softening my voice, I take a deep breath, choosing my words carefully. "Kitten, I get it. I understand how unbearable it feels, how tempting it is to find an easy way out. But this—" I glance at the pill bottle, the weight of it heavy between us, "this isn't the answer, baby. You're stronger than you think, and you're not alone in this. Our pack will get you through it. I promise." She looks up at me, her eyes brimming with tears, the faintest flicker of hope in them.

It's enough for now. Enough to keep her going.

"Alpha," she murmurs, her voice shaky, desperation clinging to every word. "I need you, Hux. I need your knot. Please."

Her plea hits me like a punch to the gut, tearing down the last of my resolve. The raw need in her voice, the way her fingers grip my shirt like I'm her lifeline—it's too much to bear. I can't leave her, not when she's begging me to stay, not when I know the consequences of denying her.

"Kitten," I say softly, brushing a strand of hair away from her sweat soaked face. "You know I'd do anything for you. But are you sure this is what you want? Vaughn and Creed can help—"

"I want *you*," she interrupts, her voice firm despite the tears still shining in her eyes. "I need my alpha."

Her words send a rush of conflicting emotions through me. The thought of being the one she turns to in her time of need fills me with a sense of pride, but there's also a nagging fear that I might fail her again.

"I just don't want to hurt you," I admit, my voice barely more than a whisper. "I would die if I hurt you."

"You won't," she assures me, her hand coming up to cup my cheek. "I think... the only way to break my heat is with an alpha knot." The weight of her words settles over me, and I realize the full extent of what she's saying.

The heat she's experiencing—it's not natural.

It's been induced by the Heat drug, a substance so potent it forces omegas into relentless cycles of heat that only an alpha's knot can break. It's a drug designed for one purpose—to breed. The breeder facilities used it to keep their omegas in a perpetual state of need, to ensure they would mate as often as possible. Without an alpha's knot, the heat doesn't just subside; it builds, intensifies, until the omega is driven to madness.

That's why the overdoses have been happening. Omegas, desperate for relief, keep taking dose after dose, not understanding that only an alpha's knot can release them from the drug's vicious grip. The thought sends a chill down my spine.

I can't let that happen to Kay. I won't.

"I'll stay with you," I vow, my voice firm with the promise of protection. "I won't leave you. Not ever again."

Her grip on me tightens, and I can see the fear slowly giving way to trust. "I need you, Hux," she whispers, her voice trembling. "Please."

"I'm here, kitten," I say, pressing a kiss to her forehead. "And I'm going to make sure you get through this."

As I lower her gently onto the bed, I can feel her body trembling, her scent thickening with the telltale signs of her heat reaching its peak. She's right—without an alpha's knot, the heat will only grow more intense, more unbearable.

I won't let it consume her. Not while I'm here.

Chapter 15
Creed

THIS PAST WEEK WITH my pack has been incredible. After Kay's heat finally broke, we all got a chance to just breathe, to be together without the constant tension and worry. The four of us have been piled into Hux's room. Even with his California king, the space isn't really big enough for three males, who all want a chance to hold our little omega. It forces us to all pile on top of each other.

But I wouldn't have it any other way.

I glance down at Kay nestled in the crook of my arm, her cheek resting on my bicep, her soft breaths tickling my skin. I study her sleeping face, dark lashes fanning out on her rosy cheeks. My heart swells with love, so intense it almost hurts. She's been through so much, yet she's here, safe and wrapped up in my arms. Vaughn is pressed along my spine, his warmth and bitter-sweet scent a steady reassurance. Hux lies with his back to us on the opposite side of Kay, his breathing even, but I can tell he's still on edge, even in sleep. He carries so much weight, always worrying about our safety, always planning the next move. I wish he could let go, even just for a little while, but I know he won't. That's just who he is, our anchor, our protector.

There's something about having them so close that soothes my omega instincts like nothing else. The challenges we've faced, the battles still to come—they all fade away in this moment. All I feel is the love I have for my pack, the bond that holds us together, stronger than anything else. I can't wait for the day we are all tied together. Bound by Hux's bite and officially known as Pack Huxley. I've never wanted anything more.

Kay murmurs something in her sleep, her brows knitting together. My jaw tightens as I watch the beginning of a nightmare start to form. I stroke her hair gently, brushing a stray lock away from her face to soothe her.

"You're safe," I breathe the words softly, the same way I always remind her, and continue to stroke my fingers along her cheek. She inhales sharply at my touch, my voice. "Rest, tiny, you're safe with your pack, baby."

She lets out a long breath, her brows smoothing, and the hand clenched into the sheets releases its tension as she settles back into sleep. My gut twists. My brother is the reason she's so tormented. He's to blame for the constant struggle of my pack and why we can't officially bond as a whole. Soon--but with my mother manipulating this entire city to cater to her beloved son, not soon enough. I grit my teeth and stare up at the ceiling, the weight of it all pressing down on me.

The next generation pack, the breeding facility, all the death and carnage my family has left in their wake. All in the name of power. It's sickening. And Stacy Bramwell. The female beta who was so desperate to gain more power in this city, by whatever means necessary, that she died because of her greed. She trusted Jordan, a Hound, and she was killed in cold blood by his men. The city held a service for her, but even then, my mother used her death to maintain her control. *"The Bramwell Sanctuary will honor her, and all those omegas who have been lost."* My mother's words echo in my mind, hollow and calculated.

But I know the truth. The Sanctuary is just another cog in the machine of manipulation and control. Another way to keep the powerful in power and the vulnerable at their mercy. And it's my family's legacy that allows it all to continue. The thought burns in my chest, a reminder of how far I've fallen from the ideals I once held.

I glance down at Kay, her peaceful face a stark contrast to the turmoil inside me. She's been through so much, more than anyone should have to endure. And yet, here she is, fighting to survive, to protect the pack we've built together. I can't help but feel a deep sense of responsibility for her suffering.

If I had been stronger, if I had walked away from my family sooner, maybe things would be different. Maybe Rebecca would still be alive, and Kay wouldn't have to live in fear of my brother, who lost his mind long ago. But those are just maybes, and they won't change the reality we face now.

Adam has to be taken out by any means necessary. Though, the fallout from that could be worse... My mother will go ballistic. We need to be ready for that. Need the Steel Serpents and any of the Hounds who don't follow Titus to back us.

My mother, my brother—they won't stop until they've destroyed everything we've built. But as long as I have breath in my body, I won't let them. I won't let them take away the family I've found here, in this pack. My beta, my omega, or my alpha.

First, break Kay free of her bond with Adam. Second, solidify the Huxley pack. After that, it doesn't matter because we will do it together.

Vaughn stirs behind me, a hardness grinding into my back that stirs my own to life. I smirk, glancing lazily over my shoulder.

"Good morning to you too," I tease.

Vaughn grinds into me again, this time with a bit more force, and both of us groan together. His breath is hot against my neck, a low growl vibrating from his chest.

"Morning," he rumbles, his voice thick with sleep and something darker, more primal.

The teasing edge in my tone fades as the heat between us simmers. I can feel the tension coiling in the air, a familiar pull that's been growing stronger ever since Kay's heat. There's a rawness in the way Vaughn touches me now, a need that mirrors my own.

"You know," I murmur, twisting slightly to meet his gaze, "if you keep that up, we're not getting out of bed today."

His lips twitch into a lazy grin. "Would that be such a bad thing?"

My smirk widens as I arch a brow. "Depends on how bad you want to take Kay to The Ring today."

That gets his attention.

Vaughn's eyes flicker with a mix of desire and determination, the same look he gets when he's about to go all in during a fight. He's been itching to train her, to take her to his family's gym. And as much as the thought of staying tangled in these sheets with him is tempting, I know we've got work to do. While they're busy, Hux and I are making Kay her own nest and meeting with the city officials to get back our liquor license so we can reopen the Den.

But that doesn't mean I can't enjoy a few more minutes of this first.

I shift, pressing back into him, earning another groan as his fingers dig into my hips. "You better make it quick, then," I murmur, letting the challenge linger in the space between us.

Vaughn doesn't hesitate. His grip tightens, and the last of our restraint frays, giving way to the heat that's been simmering between us all week. He reaches around and grabs my cock in a fierce grip, making me hiss.

"Careful, pet. Don't wake my doll up," he growls, nipping at my earlobe.

I bite down on my lip to stifle the groan building in my throat as he pumps me harder, the sensation almost too much to bear. I want to touch him too, to feel the heat of his skin under my fingers. But my arm is trapped beneath tiny, her warmth anchoring me while Vaughn's hips press into my ass with relentless force, like a couple of horny teenagers grinding against each other with our clothes still on.

But damn, it's so fucking hot.

It's a sweet torment, being completely at his mercy, unable to move, unable to do anything but take everything he's giving. My breath comes in short, ragged gasps, the pressure inside me coiling tighter and tighter, desperate for release. I can't hold back much longer, and he knows it. I feel the smirk against my ear, the way his teeth graze my skin as he leans in close, his voice a low, dangerous whisper.

"Be a good boy for me, Creed," he purrs, his hand moving faster, more insistent. "Come for me. Silently."

I nod, the command washing over me like a wave, pulling me under. My body tenses, muscles coiling as I chase the edge, the pleasure teetering on the brink of my control. Vaughn's grip tightens, and the world narrows down to the heat of his touch, the feel of his body pressed against mine, the sound of our breaths mingling in the quiet of the room.

With a final, shuddering breath, I let go, the release crashing through me in a wave so intense I see stars behind my eyes. I bite down hard on my lip, barely containing the groan that threatens to break free. My body trembles as Vaughn strokes me through it, drawing out every last bit of pleasure until I'm left gasping, spent, and sated. Vaughn's hand lingers, a gentle caress now, soothing and grounding. He presses a soft kiss to the back of my neck, his breath warm against my skin.

"Good boy," he murmurs, his voice thick with satisfaction. It's quick, intense, and when it's over, we're both left panting, hearts pounding in sync.

I close my eyes, savoring the moment. The feel of Vaughn's body still pressed against mine, the steady rhythm of Kay's breathing, and the comforting weight of our pack surrounding us is bliss.

"You drive me crazy, pet," he mutters, and I chuckle, leaning over to capture his lips in a bruising kiss, tasting the heat and satisfaction lingering on his breath. When we break apart, our eyes lock, and I see the same fire burning in his gaze—the fire that's ready for whatever comes next, that's kept us alive through every challenge my family's thrown at us. It's the same fire I see in Kay, in Hux, in myself.

The room is quiet, the morning light creeping in through the curtains, casting a soft glow over the tangle of limbs and sheets that make up our pack. I take a moment to savor it, this fleeting peace, before the day's chaos begins.

"Okay," Vaughn says. "Now you can wake her."

I grin, running my hand gently over tiny's cheek, feeling her start to stir under my touch. Her eyelashes flutter, and she mumbles something incoherent, pressing closer to my chest as if resisting the pull of consciousness.

"Morning, tiny," I murmur, my voice low and soothing. "Time to wake up baby. I hear Vaughn is going to teach you how to fight today."

She blinks up at me, her eyes still bleary with sleep, but a small smile tugs at her lips as she takes in the sight of me, of us, her pack surrounding her. There's a moment of quiet contentment before the excitement starts to creep into her expression.

"Really?" she asks, her gray eyes lighting up with a spark of anticipation. But just as quickly, she bites her bottom lip, nervousness clouding her features. "Are you going to be there too?" Her voice is soft, almost hesitant, as she looks up at me with a mix of hope and uncertainty.

I shake my head, giving her a reassuring smile. "No, tiny. Hux and I are going to build your nest today. But don't worry, you'll be in good hands with Vaughn."

She nods, though I can see the lingering apprehension in her eyes. I brush a strand of hair from her face, my touch gentle, grounding her in the moment.

"You'll do great," I add, my voice steady with conviction. "And when you're done, you'll have a nest to come back to—a place that's all yours, where you'll always be safe."

Her smile returns, softer this time but more certain. She leans into my touch, her nerves easing as she finds comfort in the promise of what's to come. A gentle peck lands on my cheek, her lips warm and reassuring.

"I can't wait to see it," she whispers, her voice soft with anticipation. Her smile grows, her rose scent filling the space around us, delicate and soothing.

Hux grumbles from his side of the bed, the sound vibrating through the mattress. I glance over to see him stretching, his eyes still half-closed. He's slow to wake, but as always, he's drawn to her warmth like a magnet. He shifts closer, his arms wrapping around tiny as he nestles his nose into the crook of her neck. His spicy scent mingles with hers, marking her in that subtle yet possessive way he always does.

"We're shopping today?" Hux's voice is thick with sleep, but there's no real complaint in it. His hands find her hips instinctively, pulling her against him as he inhales deeply, contentment softening his features.

His blue eyes meet mine over her shoulder, a playful glint in them despite the lingering drowsiness. "You're going to help me pick out all the best omega comforts, right?"

I nod, sharing in his excitement. "Of course. All the blankets, pillows, and comforts an omega could ever need."

Hux smiles gratefully, his hand slipping down to intertwine with Kay's. The thought of creating a space just for her—a nest where she can feel safe, loved, and at home—fills him with as much purpose as it does me. I can see it in the way he looks at her.

A grin spreads across my face as I watch them together. My omega and my alpha. "Time to get moving. We've got a long day ahead, lovebirds."

Tiny shifts slightly, turning her head to look up at Hux. "You're really going to build me a nest?" There's a note of wonder in her voice, a spark of excitement that makes her eyes shine.

Hux nods, pressing a soft kiss to her temple. "Anything for you, kitten. We'll make sure it's perfect—a place just for you to relax and feel safe. And we'll add a reading nook too, with all your favorite books."

Her eyes light up at the mention of the reading nook, her love for books immediately evident. "Really? A reading nook?" she asks, her voice tinged with disbelief.

Vaughn chuckles from behind me, finally joining the conversation. "Of course, doll. We know how much you love to read. It wouldn't be *your* nest without one," he says, his tone teasing but affectionate.

Her smile widens, and she looks at each of us in turn, her eyes filled with a mix of gratitude and something deeper, something that speaks to the bond we all share. "Thank you," she whispers, her voice choked with emotion. "I've never had anything like this before."

I lean in, brushing my lips against her forehead. "You deserve it, tiny. And we're going to make sure it's everything you've ever wanted. Your own little sanctuary."

Hux hums in agreement, his fingers tracing soothing patterns on her hip. "We'll fill it with all your favorite things. You'll have your own space to retreat to whenever you need it."

Vaughn chimes in, his voice warm and reassuring. "And it'll always be there for you, no matter what. A place where you can just be yourself, surrounded by the pack who loves you."

Kay's eyes glisten with unshed tears, but the smile on her face is one of pure happiness. "I'm always surrounded by my pack. I love you all too," she says softly, her voice filled with hope and acceptance.

"Then let's get a move on," I repeat softly, my heart swelling with love for her and our pack. "We've got a lot to do today and you've got a date with Vaughn." I kiss her one last time, savoring her taste on my lips. "See you later, tiny. We'll make the perfect nest, just like you deserve."

CHAPTER 16
Kaylani

S LIDING INTO THE CAB of Creed's pickup, I slam the door shut, feeling the familiar jolt of the truck's interior. The early morning sun filters through the windshield, casting a warm glow over everything. Vaughn's comforting, chocolatey scent wraps around me, a balm to my frayed nerves. I inhale deeply, trying to steady myself. The lingering effects of my heat have made me even more sensitive to my pack's scents.

I swallow hard, nerves fluttering in my stomach as I brace for the day ahead. Excitement bubbles beneath the surface, barely contained. Today marks our first sparring session and the first time I'm leaving the Den since Hux brought me home when my heat started. The thought of stepping out into the world again, of testing my strength, fills me with a mix of anticipation and anxiety.

The idea of eventually confronting Adam head-on is terrifying.

The engine roars to life, a deep rumble that vibrates through my seat, and Vaughn expertly guides the truck away from the curb. The soft morning light filters through the windows, making the interior glow with a gentle warmth. I take a moment to study his profile—the strong lines of his jaw, the way his tattooed arm dangles casually out the open window. His other hand grips the steering wheel with a relaxed confidence, his knuckles barely showing any strain. It's a small thing, but that ease, that control, does something to me that makes my heart race.

The thought of his strong, tattooed arms wrapped around me as he instructs me to break free sends heat to my core. I squeeze my thighs together, trying to stem off the ache I can't deny. Without Creed's teasing banter diffusing the tension, it's just me and Vaughn tonight. And it will be that much harder to keep my hands off of him.

I watch the passing lights and shadows as the truck rolls down the quiet morning streets, trying to steady my nerves. The truck's rumble and the soft hum of the engine are the only sounds that break the silence stretching between us.

I steal another glance at Vaughn. His features are highlighted by the morning light—strong jawline, stubbled chin, everything about the beta screams rough around the edges. But despite everything, there's a softer side to him too, a warmth that makes me feel like I'm in capable hands.

"So, where are we going?" I ask nervously, trying to keep the tremor out of my voice. "The docks?"

I gnaw on my bottom lip, the idea of seeing Vaughn fight again more tempting than I'd like to admit. Memories of the last time flash through my mind—his precise movements, the raw power behind each strike.

A shiver runs down my spine.

Vaughn chuckles, clearly enjoying the heat in my eyes, and a blush coats my cheeks as I wait for him to talk.

"You want to know if we're going to the docks?" He gives me that lazy grin again, and for a moment, I forget to breathe. "Nah, doll, we've got something different in mind today. But first a little pit-stop for breakfast. Can't train on an empty stomach."

My heart skips a beat, and I blink, trying to process his words. Vaughn is so rarely like this—teasing, almost playful—and it throws me off balance. "Pit-stop?" I echo, curiosity piqued. "Where?"

He glances over at me, his eyes twinkling with a mischief that's so out of character it makes my pulse jump. I do love this side of my beta, but it's also putting me even more on edge than I was when I got into the truck.

"Well, you missed meeting my family when you were at your aunt's house. Remember?" His tone is light, but there's an edge to it, a reminder of the chaos I caused by leaving Bex's funeral the way I did. "My uncle has been asking about you."

My eyes practically bulge out of my head at the idea of meeting his family—more specifically, his uncle Viper. The MC lives just on the outskirts of town, a world I've heard about but never ventured into. The thought of stepping into that world, of meeting the infamous Viper Calhan, sends a jolt of adrenaline through me.

"Now?" I squeak, the word coming out higher-pitched than I intended. My mind races with possibilities, none of them particularly reassuring. "Vaughn, I—" I cut myself off, not even sure what to say. Meeting Viper?

The idea is both terrifying and intriguing, and I'm not sure how to feel about it.

Vaughn laughs again, this time a full, rich sound that makes my insides twist in the best way. But even the delicious sound can't stop the knots from forming in my stomach.

"Relax, doll. Viper's not as scary as everyone says." He pauses, a wicked glint in his eyes. "Well, maybe a little."

Vaughn winks. He fucking winks at me. Teasing me.

"Don't joke!" I say, a nervous laugh escaping my lips. "You're not making this any easier, you know."

"Don't worry so much, doll. You're with me. Nothing's gonna happen that you can't handle." The weight of his hand lingers. "Plus, my unc is going to love you, Kay. Just like I do."

I smile softly, my mouth suddenly dry. I give him a nod, more to convince myself than anything, and try to shake off the nerves. If Vaughn says I can handle it, then I believe him. But as the truck speeds down the road, carrying us closer to whatever awaits, I can't help but wonder what meeting Viper will be like. Meeting Vaughn's family, his MC, is a whole new level of intimidating. I've heard stories about them—stories that would make anyone nervous. But there's also a flicker of curiosity. I've wanted to understand this side of Vaughn, the world he comes from, ever since I first met him. But I need to know what I'm walking into.

"Okay I'm meeting the Steel Serpents. No pressure," I murmur before turning to face him again. "So tell me where we are going, then. It's only fair." I know I'm whining at this point, but I can't seem to stop myself.

Vaughn chuckles softly at my tone, that lazy grin never leaving his face. "We're headed to their clubhouse."

My hand grips the seat belt tighter as I gaze out the window, the cityscape blurring past in a mosaic of early morning light. The sun has barely risen, casting a soft, golden hue across the streets as we leave the familiar hustle behind in the city. But I can't focus on anything else but the tangled knots of anxiety. The nerves about meeting the Serpents have nothing to do with their reputation as a motorcycle club, but everything to do with them being Vaughn's family.

The truck rumbles steadily, its old engine growling with each bump in the road. We drive through quiet suburbs, and my thoughts whirl with every passing streetlight. The world outside is waking up, but inside the truck, inside my head, tension swirls and no amount of deep breathing seems to soothe it.

The houses slowly bleed into a wooded area and the truck seems to hit every pothole in the bumpy dirt road. We turn down a random dirt trail where tall, overgrown grass flanks the path. As we crest a curve, a massive house comes into view.

The house Vaughn grew up in.

The sprawling porch is adorned with mismatched rocking chairs and hanging plants, each one showing signs of years of use. A few people are milling about outside; a young woman in a sunhat waters a row of potted plants, while a burly man in a leather jacket leans against a pickup truck, chatting animatedly with someone inside. Near the porch, a group of kids are playing catch, their laughter ringing out across the lawn.

It's all a bit overwhelming. I wasn't expecting this many people. Do they all live on the Serpents compound? I blow out a long breath, taking it all in before gazing up at Vaughn, pleading for reassurance.

Looks like I am about to walk into the snake's den. Here goes nothing.

CHAPTER 17
Vaughn

I shift the truck into park, the old engine rumbling to a stop. Kay's face is a portrait of nerves and determination. I know this is a big step for her, meeting my family, and I can see the anxiety etched into her features. I want to make this as easy as possible for her.

I reach over and cradle her cheek, my thumb brushing gently across her skin. "Do you trust me?" I ask, my voice low and earnest. I can't help but feel a protective instinct flare up—she's important to me, and I need her to know that she's safe here.

Her gray eyes meet mine, and I can see the vulnerability behind them. "Yes. Of course I trust you," she replies, her voice soft. Relief washes over me at her response.

It's what I needed to hear.

"Then hear me when I say this, Kay. You are perfect. You have nothing to worry about when you're here. You're safe here." I lean in and press a tender kiss to her lips, trying to impart as much warmth and reassurance as I can. I know it's working when I feel her relax slightly under my touch, the tension in her shoulders easing.

It's a good sign.

I watch as her gaze shifts to the imposing house and the lineup of motor-cycles. "Ready?" I ask, with a reassuring smile. I want her to feel supported, to know that we're in this together.

She nods, her expression steadier. "Yeah, I'm ready."

I open my door and step out of the truck, feeling the familiar thud of my boots on the ground. The early morning sun warms the porch, casting a golden light over the place. It's my childhood home, and I want Kay to feel like she belongs here too. I reach back and take her hand, giving it a reassuring squeeze. Her steps are hesitant but resolute as we walk up the porch steps. I can hear the sounds of my family inside—the clatter of dishes, the murmur of voices, and the occasional burst of laughter.

Pushing open the front door, I let the familiar creak echo through the house. "Morning, unc!" I call out, my voice carrying through the space. I can't help but feel a bit of excitement as we enter, hoping my uncle and the rest of the family will make a good impression on Kay.

"In here!" My uncle's deep, gravelly voice responds, coming from beyond the living room.

I lead Kay through the entryway, my hand firmly holding hers. As we round the corner into the kitchen, the scene opens up in front of us: my family gathered around the large wooden table, the room buzzing with morning energy. My uncle stands at the stove, flipping hashbrowns with practiced ease. He's got that rugged, salt-and-pepper look—years of life etched into his face. I notice the way he glances up at us, his eyes first landing on me before shifting to Kay. She squirms a bit under his scrutiny and my chest tightens a little as I watch her, wishing I could take away her nerves. But I know she's strong, and I hope she can see that my family is welcoming and warm.

"Morning, everyone!" I announce, "I'd like you all to meet Kaylani."

The room's attention shifts to Kay, and I feel a surge of pride as well as relief as I see my family greet her with smiles and nods. I watch as the initial tension in her posture begins to ease, replaced by a more relaxed, welcoming demeanor. This is what I wanted—to see Kay feel comfortable and accepted.

"Kaylani, this is my Uncle Viper," I say, pointing to the rugged man at the stove. "And this is Ghost, my best friend." I gesture towards Ghost, who's already seated at the table, a half-eaten plate of food in front of him.

Viper gives Kay a warm smile. "Nice to meet you, Kaylani. Vaughn's told us a lot about you." His voice is gruff but kind, and there's a twinkle of amusement in his eyes as he adds, "Don't let Vaughn's stories scare you off. We aren't that bad."

I blow out a breath, thankful that he isn't giving her a hard time like he had with Creed.

Ghost looks up from his plate, offering Kay a friendly smile. "Yeah, nice to meet you Kay. Don't worry too much, we're all pretty laid-back here."

Kay returns their smiles, her nerves visibly easing. "It's nice to meet you both," she replies, her voice soft but sincere.

Viper nods and gestures to an empty seat at the table. "Why don't you and Vaughn take a seat? Breakfast is almost ready."

As Kay and I settle into our seats, I can see her shoulders relax. I lean into her and murmur, "See? I told you. You were worrying about nothing, doll."

She looks up at me, an adorable blush coating her cheeks. "There's so many people. It's a bit overwhelming."

I nod, squeezing her hand under the table for reassurance. "Most will be out of here once Unc passes out breakfast. Then it'll be just us."

Viper crosses the room, carrying a platter of food and a couple of plates. "Help yourself, Kaylani. We've got plenty."

Kay thanks him shyly, her hand finding mine again under the table. I can feel her grip tightening slightly, her nerves still a little frayed despite the warm welcome. I give her a reassuring squeeze, hoping to offer some comfort.

Ghost turns to face us, a smile spreading across his face. "So, I hear you're going to The Ring today."

Kay glances between us, a piece of bacon halfway to her lips. She swallows awkwardly before responding. "Oh. Um... I don't know." Her gaze flickers up to me for reassurance.

I nod, giving her an encouraging smile. "Yep, though I hadn't told Kay yet. What better place to start your training than the MC gym? So eat up. You'll need your energy for what I have planned for you."

The blush on her cheeks deepens, traveling down her chest, a mix of embarrassment and excitement. Damn, she's adorable. I can't help but feel a swell of pride. This is a big step for her, and seeing her embrace it with such raw, genuine emotion makes me even more determined to support her.

Viper sits down next to Ghost, taking a moment to pile food onto his plate before he speaks. "You're going to do great, Kaylani. My nephew's a hell of a teacher."

Kay's eyes dart between Viper, Ghost, and me, a flicker of surprise crossing her face. The kitchen is quieter now, everyone else having left to let us enjoy our breakfast in peace. She hesitates before responding, her voice tinged with a mix of hope and uncertainty. "I hope so. It would be nice not to feel so helpless anymore."

Viper sets his fork down and leans back slightly, his gaze steady on Kay. A silence falls over the table, its weight punctuated by the distant hum of activity outside. "Kaylani," Viper begins, his voice taking on a gruff, contemplative tone. She stiffens slightly, her shoulders bunching, before meeting his gaze. "Do you know why this MC was created?"

Kay glances briefly at Ghost, who offers a reassuring nod, before turning her attention back to Viper. She shakes her head slowly, a touch of confusion in her eyes. "No, I don't."

Viper's expression softens, though his voice remains resolute. "It was created to protect those who need it. To offer a refuge in times of turmoil."

He gestures around the room, as if to underscore the sentiment. "The Serpents have agreed to help secure the Den and assist in reopening it to the public, to ensure our city has a safe space for those who need it. I hear your brother Shade has also enlisted a few Hounds for support."

Kay's brows shoot up in surprise, her eyes widening. "Yes, he did mention that to me," she says softly, her voice carrying a note of surprise and uncertainty.

Viper leans in, his gaze unwavering. "So, given everything you've heard and experienced, do you think it's worth the risk? To be part of something that stands for protection and safety?"

I watch Kay's expression shift from uncertainty to contemplation. She nods slowly, her voice gaining strength. "Yes. I think it's worth it. It's important to stand up and fight for a better future, even if it's risky."

Viper's gaze softens as he sees the resolve hardening in Kay's eyes, a glimmer of determination that makes me swell with pride. He nods approvingly and leans forward slightly, his voice warm. "That's the spirit. When you step into my gym today, remember that. Remember why this is worth the risk. It's not just about training—it's about standing up for yourself and what you believe in."

Kay absorbs his words, her expression hardening. "I will," she replies, her voice steady. "I'll keep that in mind."

Viper's nod is encouraging. "Good. You'll do just fine. You've got the heart for it, and that's what counts."

I reach over, giving Kay's hand a reassuring squeeze. I know today will be a challenge, but I'm confident she's ready to face it head-on.

As the breakfast conversation shifts back to lighter topics, I glance at Kay, my heart swelling with pride. This is more than just a training day; it's the beginning of a new chapter for her—and for us.

CHAPTER 18
Kaylani

A SURGE OF APPREHENSION washes over me as Vaughn pulls up outside the weathered brick building. We ended up hanging out at the MC compound until late afternoon. It had been surprisingly pleasant getting to know his family. They were rough around the edges, but more welcoming than I had anticipated. I glance up at the neon sign, which reads, "The Ring" and my throat tightens, a knot of nerves settling in.

"Ready?" Vaughn asks, his voice gentle but firm.

"I'm nervous," I admit, my voice barely a whisper.

Vaughn cuts the engine and turns to face me, his gaze intense, yet unreadable. "You got this, doll," he says, his voice low and steady. "But if you'd rather just go home, that's okay too."

The sincerity in his voice tugs at something deep inside me. I take a shaky breath, looking at the building looming ahead. It's more than just nerves;

it's the fear of stepping into the unknown, of confronting my own limitations.

I'm a healer, not a fighter.

Though I'm not much of a nurse anymore—that part of myself feels so distant. Who knows, maybe one day I'll go back to Sterling Hospital, but right now, I'm not ready to face it. But I know I need to face this. Face Adam and these lingering nightmares. I can't take it anymore, feeling so helpless and vulnerable. I need to fight back. For me. For Bex. For all those omegas that are still 'missing'.

I meet Vaughn's gaze. "No. I'm not going home," I say, my voice firmer. "I *need* to do this. I *want* to do this, Vaughn. To fight against everything that has ever made me feel weak. I need to take back my power."

A slow, approving smile spreads across Vaughn's face, and he reaches over, giving my hand a reassuring squeeze. "That's my girl. Let's go show this place what you're made of."

As we push open the door, the smell of sweat and old leather hits me. Inside, Vaughn leads me to a corner of the gym where a training area is set up. He turns to face me, his expression focused. "Let's start with some basics," Vaughn says, a hint of excitement in his voice. "You're going to learn how to hold your ground, Kay."

"The place is closed?" I question, raising an eyebrow.

He nods. "Yeah, I figured you'd rather not have an audience. So I asked Viper to close it down for us."

A smile tugs at my lips at how thoughtful Vaughn truly is. This place is completely out of my comfort zone and not having an audience will definitely help. With Vaughn by my side and the gym all to ourselves, I feel a flicker of hope igniting amidst the fear.

Vaughn gestures toward the training area, where mats and equipment are arranged. His eyes gleam with a mix of pride and anticipation as he begins to guide me through the basics.

"Alright, doll," Vaughn's voice is low and commanding as he steps closer in the dimly lit corner of the gym. "Let's start with your stance."

Suddenly, my mouth goes dry, the sight of him in this environment almost too much. Vaughn circles to stand behind me, and I'm acutely aware of his proximity. I can practically feel his heat against my back. His hands gently guide my shoulders and hips into the proper alignment, sending a shiver down my spine. I catch a whiff of his scent, a mix of sweat and chocolate, and I bite back a groan. My senses are heightened, the awareness of him making my thoughts foggy. Despite my efforts to focus on the lesson, my mind wanders to the magnetic pull I feel toward Vaughn. There's something about his confidence, his intensity, that draws me in. And right now, I want nothing more than for him to take me down onto the mat for a completely different reason.

"Like this?" I ask, my voice tinged with uncertainty.

Vaughn circles around me, his dark gaze locking with mine, a smirk playing at the corners of his lips.

"Almost," he murmurs, his warm breath brushing against my cheek. "You've got to loosen up, Kay. Relax."

I inhale deeply, trying to steady my racing heartbeat. Relaxing feels impossible with Vaughn so close, but I try to follow his instructions, wanting to impress him.

"Good girl," Vaughn's voice is husky, his eyes holding mine for a lingering moment.

A shiver courses through me at the praise. I steal a glance at Vaughn, searching for any sign that he's as affected by our closeness as I am.

"Now, let's work on your punches," Vaughn says, stepping back slightly to give me room.

I mimic his stance, throwing a jab into the air. "Like this?" I ask, trying to ignore the way Vaughn's eyes roam over my form, assessing and lingering.

Vaughn nods, a playful glint in his eyes. "Not bad, doll. But remember, it's not just about the size of the person. It's how you use your whole body to deliver the punch. Your power comes from the ground up, not just your arms."

He steps closer, and the heat between us intensifies as his hand gently guides my hip. His touch is intimate, and I have to force myself not to react to the heat of his fingers.

"Use your body weight to your advantage. Start with your feet, plant them firmly. As you throw the punch, rotate your hips and shoulders, letting the energy flow from your core through your arm. It's a full-body movement, not just an arm swing."

I struggle to focus on his instructions, feeling the warmth of his hand on my hip. Every fiber of my being wants to react to his touch, but I force myself to concentrate on the technique. I shift my weight, pivoting on my heel and trying to integrate his guidance.

"Good," Vaughn murmurs, his voice low and approving. "Feel the difference? It's about channeling that energy effectively. The punch is powerful not because of brute strength, but because you've harnessed the power of your entire body."

I gnaw on my lip as I concentrate on what he is saying, and throw my body into the next jab. "Better?" I ask breathily, feeling the burn in my muscles.

"Much better," Vaughn confirms, his gaze intense. "Keep practicing. The more you integrate your whole body, the stronger your punches will become."

I blow out a breath and attempt the movement a few more times before adding my left hand to the motion. But it feels awkward and stiff, lacking fluidity, and I struggle to get it just right.

Vaughn chuckles, stepping closer once more. "Getting there," he murmurs, his voice husky. "But I think you can do better."

Our bodies are inches apart now, the heat between us undeniable. My pulse quickens as I feel Vaughn's presence, his scent overwhelming my senses. I meet his gaze, my own filled with determination.

"Show me," I challenge in a soft whisper. I'm not so sure I'm talking about how to throw a punch anymore. He takes a couple of steps back, and I'm grateful for the momentary distance. I take in a few deep breaths, watching as he walks across the room to a shelf with boxing gloves and various gear. I wipe the sweat from my brow, taking a swig of water before setting it down on the edge of the mat.

"Alright, let's see what you've got," Vaughn says with a smirk, holding up his gloved hands.

I frown. "What am I supposed to do, punch you?" My eyes bounce between Vaughn's hands and his face. Suddenly, I feel unsure. As an omega, I've never been much of a fighter, especially not with my fists. How do I admit that I don't even know how to hold my fist properly? What if I break my thumb or something? My mind reels with thoughts, and I steady myself with a deep breath.

"Come on, Kay, put your hands up like I showed you," Vaughn encourages softly.

I blow out a breath, a piece of hair falling into my face from my ponytail, brushing against my cheek. Bouncing back and forth for a moment, I brace myself before throwing the first punch into his gloved hand. The impact feels solid, and a surge of power flows through me. I pivot my weight, using my body to drive the next punch with more force, landing a stronger hit against his gloves.

"That felt good," I admit. A zing I've never felt before courses through me, and I grin. Vaughn's eyes widen slightly with surprise, and he raises his brow in approval.

"Good job doll." I see a flicker of admiration in his gaze, and a swell of pride rises within me. I let out a breathless laugh.

"Alright. I'm calling it," Vaughn says, his voice edged with a new note of respect. "Let's take a break."

I nod, taking wobbly steps toward my water bottle, collapsing onto the mat in a heap when I reach it. Vaughn comes over and sits down beside me, and for a moment, we sit in comfortable silence. A thin sheen of sweat gathers on his brow, a drop pooling and traveling down the side of his sharp jaw. My eyes track the movement, and I have this sudden urge to taste the saltiness on my tongue. There is just something about my betas taste that is addicting.

Vaughn's eyes darken as they meet mine, a hint of lust seeping into his dark chocolate gaze. A smile spreads across his handsome face. "Alright, doll. One more time and I'll give you exactly what you've been begging me for the last few hours, right here on the mat."

My throat bobs at the implication. "Deal?" he asks, his eyes ghosting over my heated skin.

"Deal."

CHAPTER 19

Vaughn

S ITTING ON THE MAT, I glance over at Kaylani. Her skin glistens with
a sheen of sweat, her hair a tangled mess plastered to her forehead.
We've been here for hours, it's well past nightfall and time for us to call it
a night. Her lips are slightly parted as she tries to catch her breath. She's
petite and the thought of her facing someone like Adam alone fills me with
dread. How do you tell someone you love that you're scared they're not
strong enough?

She wants to learn self-defense, and I'm so damn proud of her for taking
that step. Yet, the worry gnaws at me, a relentless reminder of the world's
brutality. Adam is a monster, a force of nature, and I can't bear the thought
of Kaylani facing him alone again. The fear in my chest is a constant ache,
but I push it down, focusing on what I can do to help her.

I pull out my favorite blade from my pocket, the one I carry everywhere.
It's the only thing I have left from my mom. The handle is worn from years
of use, the blade sharp and deadly. Holding it in my hand, I feel a rush of
memories and emotions. This knife has been my constant companion, a

symbol of strength and resilience. Now, I'm about to entrust it to Kay, and the weight of that decision hits me hard.

Kaylani looks at the blade curiously, her eyes wide. "What's that?"

I take a deep breath, feeling the weight of the past pressing down on me. "This knife... it was my mom's. And I want you to have it. She gave it to me before she was killed by the Hounds. It's been with me through everything."

Her eyes soften, and she reaches out, her fingers gently tracing the handle. "I'm so sorry, Vaughn."

I nod, swallowing hard. "She was a strong woman. She fought hard, but the Hounds... they don't play fair. They killed her, and losing his sister is what pushed Viper to form the Steel Serpents. That's why there's always been a rift between the gang and the MC. They've been at odds with them ever since."

Kaylani looks at the knife, her expression thoughtful. "Do you miss her?"

"Every day," I admit, my voice thick with emotion. "But having this knife... It's like having a piece of her with me. It's kept me safe, kept me grounded."

Kaylani looks up at me, her eyes filled with determination and fear. "Why are you giving it to me, then?"

I take a deep breath, trying to steady my voice. "Because I want you to have something to protect yourself with if..." I take her hand and place her fingers firmly around the handle. "If you get the chance to stab him, Kaylani, promise me you won't stop."

Tears well up in her eyes, and she shakes her head. "You don't think I can fight him off, do you?"

I reach out, cupping her cheek with my hand. "It's not that, Kay. It's just... Adam is so much bigger than you. If anything happened to you, I wouldn't be able to bear it. This way, you have something to defend yourself with. You have to be smarter than him, doll." I shake her slightly. "If you get the chance, stab him until you can't lift your arms. *Promise me.*"

She looks down at the knife, her fingers trembling. "I don't know if I can do it, Vaughn."

"You can," I say, my voice breaking. "You have to. I can't always be there to protect you, but this... this can be your protector. You want back your power? This is it."

She looks up at me, her eyes a mix of determination and fear. "I'll try. For you, for Bex, for all of us."

I pull her into my arms, holding her tightly. "That's all I ask. Just promise me you'll use it if you have to."

"I promise," she whispers, her voice choked with emotion.

I hold her for a long time, the gravity of our situation pressing down on us. I want to protect her from everything, to keep her safe from all the horrors of the world. But I know I can't do that. All I can do is give her the tools she needs to defend herself and hope that she's strong enough to use them.

"Tell me about your mom," she says softly, her fingers tracing the outline of the knife.

I take a deep breath, memories flooding back. "She was a good woman. Strong, kind. She taught me everything I know about fighting, about survival. This knife... it was hers. She gave it to me when I was just a kid, told me to always keep it with me, to always be ready. It's kept me safe, kept me grounded. And now, I hope it protects you just as fiercely."

She nods, her fingers tightening around the handle. "I'll keep it safe, Vaughn. I promise."

I smile, my heart swelling with love for her. "I know you will, doll."

We sit there in silence for a while, the weight of our emotions settling around us. I can see the determination in her eyes, the fire that burns within her. She's stronger than she knows, stronger than she believes. And I'll do everything in my power to help her see that, to help her believe in herself.

"Vaughn," she says softly, breaking the silence.

"Yeah?"

"Thank you. For everything. For believing in me, for trusting me with this."

I reach out, taking her hand in mine. "Always."

She smiles, and it's like a ray of sunshine breaking through the clouds. At that moment, I know we'll get through this. We'll face whatever comes our way, together. Kaylani is a survivor and no matter what happens, I'll always be there for her. To protect her. To love her.

"Let's call it a day, *my little fighter*," I say finally, my heart swelling with pride.

CHAPTER 20
Kaylani

HUX AND I STEP out of his bedroom, and my eyes immediately lock onto the closed door across the hall—my room, my nest. A surge of excitement floods through me, leaving me feeling giddy and exhilarated. The idea of having a nest, something I've never had before, makes my heart race with anticipation.

"When do I get to see my nest?" I ask, trying to hide my impatience. "It's been a week since you and Creed went shopping! I'm practically bursting with curiosity."

Hux chuckles softly, a warm, easy sound that makes his eyes crinkle with amusement. "So impatient," he teases, a smirk playing on his lips. "Just wait for Creed and Vaughn, they need to be here too."

I pout, crossing my arms. "Oh, come on! Why do they need to be here for me to see it? Please?"

He throws his head back, laughing heartily. "Come get me as soon as they get back, kitten, and we can all go in together."

"Why can't I go in now? All week I've seen boxes being brought up here and taken inside. I'm dying," I say dramatically

A dark, almost predatory glint flashes in his eyes, making my pulse quicken. "I promise, it'll be worth the wait."

I glance wistfully at the closed door, sighing dramatically. "Okay, fine. I'll come get you when they're back."

Hux steps closer, closing the distance between us. His lips brush mine in a soft, lingering kiss, his beard scraping gently across my lips. The sensation sends a shiver down my spine, the kiss is tender, yet brimming with a hint of something more intense that leaves me breathless.

With one final, lingering touch, Hux pulls away, his eyes still locked on mine. "I'll see you soon, Kay."

Hux's gaze remains fixed on me, filled with warmth and promise. He chuckles softly before he turns and heads towards his office. The warmth of his kiss still lingers on my lips, leaving me with a flutter of anticipation. As he disappears down the stairs, I turn my attention back to the loft.

My home.

The once-bare wall in the living room is now covered with a series of monitors, a new addition Pixie installed recently. They offer a small comfort, allowing me to keep an eye on everything downstairs, though they also serve as a stark reminder of the challenges we face.

I move to the kitchen table and sit down, feeling the cool metal of the knife Vaughn gave me pressing reassuringly against my hip, tucked securely against my waistband. Creed got me a holster for it and I haven't put the knife down since he handed it to me. Having it close makes me feel safer, like I'm carrying a part of my pack with me.

Candi is at the counter, pouring herself a cup of coffee. The rich aroma fills the air, its comforting scent contrasting with the lingering tension from earlier. She turns to me, her eyes twinkling with mischief. "About time my growly brother told you how he feels," she teases, her voice light.

I chuckle, shaking my head. "He didn't exactly *tell* me... more like showed me."

Her smile widens as she joins me at the table, sliding a cup of coffee across to me. "Well, that's Hux for you. He's never been good with words, but when it comes to actions... well, he's all in."

I take a sip of the coffee, letting its warmth spread through me, offering a brief respite from the anxious flutter in my chest. "Yeah, he really is. And the nest... I can't believe they're making me one. It feels so surreal."

Candi leans back in her chair, her expression softening. "He's been planning it for a while, you know. Ever since you came back, he wanted to do something special for you. I think it's his way of showing how much you mean to him."

Touched, I smile. "I can't wait to see it. They made me promise not to peek until they're all back, though."

"Typical," Candi says with a grin. "They want it to be perfect. Hux may act all tough, but when it comes to you, he's got a soft spot a mile wide."

Her words warm me from the inside out. It's hard to grasp just how much they care about me, but whenever it hits me I feel on top of the world. "I'm lucky to have you all."

Candi's smile dims slightly as she glances at the monitors. "We've still got a lot to do before opening night next Friday. The Den's coming together, but there's always more to prepare. And... I'm worried about how the Hounds will respond. They're not going to be happy about us staking our claim here and how it will affect the Bramwell Sanctuary."

The mention of the Hounds sends a shiver down my spine. "I've been thinking about that too. Do you think they'll come after us?"

Candi sighs, running a hand through her hair. "I wish I could say no, but we both know how they operate. They're not going to let us have this territory without a fight. But we're stronger together, and we're prepared. That's what all this is for," she gestures toward the monitors. "We're not going to be caught off guard."

I nod, feeling a mix of determination and unease. "I'm ready to do whatever it takes to keep this place safe. This is our home."

Candi reaches across the table, her hand enveloping mine in a reassuring squeeze. "I'm glad my best friend and my brother have you, Kay. Owen has softened up since you came into our lives."

I squeeze her hand back, a surge of solidarity filling me. "We'll make it work. Together."

She lets go and takes a deep breath. "Anyway, enough of the heavy stuff. What's your plan for the day?"

I lean back, thinking about the tasks ahead. "I'm waiting for Creed and Vaughn to get back with the liquor shipment. After that, I'm really just excited to see the nest Hux and Creed made for me. I've been trying to keep busy so I don't break my promise and sneak a peek."

Candi laughs softly. "It's going to be worth the wait, I promise. As for me, I'm putting out the new shipment of liquor today, so I guess we're both waiting for them to get back. We need to get everything ready for the grand re-opening. It's only nine days away now!"

I nod, anticipation building inside me. "We're so close. I can't wait to see everything come together. I talked to Serenity, even though she's five months pregnant her alpha said she could come."

Candi's grin mirrors my excitement. "I'm excited too. It's going to be a night to remember."

As we sip our coffee, the back camera triggers, letting us know someone is here. I glance at the screen, not seeing Creed's truck yet but knowing that they are back. The thought sends excitement coursing through me. A smile spreads across my face, excitement bubbling up. "I think I'll go meet them. Maybe hurry them along."

Candi chuckles, a playful glint in her eyes. "You tell them, girl. You've waited long enough for somewhere to call your own, and they need to stop making you wait."

I laugh along with her, feeling a deep sense of warmth and belonging. "I couldn't agree more." With that, I set my coffee down and head toward the back door, eager to see them. And finally get to see the nest they've been working so hard on.

CHAPTER 21
Vaughn

PULLING UP IN FRONT of the Den, Creed throws the truck in reverse, one hand on the back headrest as he expertly backs into the parking spot. He aims the tailgate so that it's near the entrance, making it easier to unload the boxes. I watch his profile, admiring the ease with which he handles the vehicle. The way he maneuvers the truck with such confidence—damn, why is that so hot?

Creed catches me watching him, a smirk tugging on his lips. "Like what you see?" he teases, his voice low and playful.

"Shut up," I grumble, though a smile creeps onto my face despite myself. He reaches over to squeeze my knee, his touch warm and comforting.

"You know you love it," he murmurs, eyes sparkling with affection.

"Maybe I do," I admit, unable to resist teasing him back.

"Damn right you do."

Despite the easy banter between us, a gnawing guilt lingers in the back of my mind. I can't shake the feeling that I've hurt him too much, that the bond we once had will always be stronger than the one we have now. The absence of my mark on his neck is a constant reminder that he's not fully mine anymore.

Sometimes I wonder if he'd be better off without me.

"Hey," he says softly, his hand reaching out to stroke my stubbled jaw. "What's going on, Vaughn? Talk to me."

I meet his green eyes, my brows furrowed in concern. He gently strokes a thumb back and forth along my jaw, patiently waiting for me to speak. "I'm so sorry for everything—"

Creed shakes his head rapidly, his blond hair momentarily tousled before falling back into place. "Stop. Stop apologizing. I'm over it all, okay? I just want our pack together and safe."

His words catch me off guard, the sincerity in his voice cutting through my self-doubt. "But I—" I begin, my throat tightening with emotion.

Creed leans closer, his forehead touching mine. "I love you, Vaughn," he breathes, his caramel scent enveloping me, making my head spin.

"God, you smell so good," I growl, my hands finding their way to the base of his neck.

Creed chuckles softly against my lips, his breath warm and teasing. He's so close, teasingly close. Just a hair's breadth from kissing me. I groan softly, unable to resist any longer. I close the gap between us, pressing my lips to his in a kiss that speaks of longing, forgiveness, and the deep bond we still share despite everything.

He responds eagerly, his arms wrapping around me, pulling me closer. The kiss deepens, our mouths moving together in a slow, passionate rhythm. It's a moment of reconnecting, of reaffirming our love and commitment.

When we finally pull back, Creed rests his forehead against mine, breathing heavily. "I love you too," I rasp, my voice husky with desire.

With a wicked grin, his hand trails down to the bulge in my jeans, teasing me with light strokes over the fabric. I shudder under his touch, but he pulls away with a chaste kiss, leaving me groaning in protest.

"Let's get this all inside, then get our pack upstairs to Kay's nest. Then we can have some real fun," he says, with that sexy grin I love so much returning to his handsome face.

"Tease," I grumble without any real heat. I get out of the truck and slam the door harder than I intended, immediately cringing at the sound. "Oops."

Creed just chuckles. "Easy there, Hulk. I like this truck. Be nice to her."

"Sorry," I mumble, my cheeks heating with embarrassment. I didn't mean to slam the door, but Creed makes me so damn crazy I can't think sometimes.

We each grab a box from the back of the truck and head toward the Den's doors. Creed strides ahead, his posture relaxed and confident, and I can't help but admire the way he carries himself. It's so effortless, like the world doesn't weigh him down the way it does me. The ease with which he moves is something I've always envied.

He glances back at me, catching my eye with a soft smile that makes my heart skip a beat. His blond hair is tucked back into his hoodie, a few loose strands framing his face, and for a moment, all I want is to reach out and touch him, to feel that warmth and reassurance that only Creed can give me.

We reach the doors, and Creed balances his box on his hip, freeing one hand to pull open the heavy entrance. The scent of fresh paint and new wood wafts out. Candi and Hux have done a lot this past week to get the den ready for next Friday's re-opening.

"Honey, we're home!" Creed yells dramatically, making me snicker despite the heaviness in my chest. He always knows how to lighten the mood, how to make me smile even when I'm drowning in my own thoughts. "After you," he says, holding the door open for me with a playful bow.

"Such a gentleman, pet," I purr.

I set my box down on one of the tables, the wood cool against my fingers as I linger for a moment, lost in thought. Creed does the same, but instead of moving on, he watches me, his gaze intense and searching.

"You okay?" he asks, his voice gentle, cutting through the heavy silence of the room.

I nod, but the words stick in my throat, the weight of everything pressing down on me again. "Yeah, just... thinking."

Thinking about everything we've been through, about the scars we both carry, visible and invisible. About how much I want—no, need—to fix everything, to be what they all deserve, to make our pack whole with Hux and Kay.

Creed steps closer, his presence grounding me in a way nothing else can. He doesn't say anything, just reaches out to take my hand, his thumb brushing soothing circles over my knuckles. The simple gesture is enough to ease the tension coiled in my chest, a reminder that no matter how much I doubt myself, Creed is here, steady and unwavering.

"We're almost there, Vaughn," he murmurs, his voice steady and reassuring. "Whatever happens, we've got each other. That's all that matters. And for the record... I forgive you for everything... You know that, don't you?"

His words sink into me, wrapping around the hurt and guilt like a balm. He's right. We've been through hell and back, but we're still standing. Still fighting. And as long as we have our pack, we can face whatever comes next. I just have to believe that, one day, I'll be able to solidify our bond again, to feel that connection snap into place.

And when that day comes, I'll be ready, no matter what it takes.

We head back to the truck for another round of boxes. The sun is high in the sky, casting a warm, golden light over everything, making the day feel almost too peaceful, too normal. With the Den nearly ready to open and our pack finally finding its footing again. With Kay getting the nest she deserves and Creed finally forgiving me, everything feels brighter.

It's hard to believe that anything could go wrong on a day like this.

We each grab another box and I head back toward the door, Creed right on my heels. Just as we reach the entrance, a piercing scream rips through the air, shattering the silence. I freeze, the sound cutting straight through me. And for a split second, everything goes silent. Creed's box slips from his grasp, hitting the ground with a loud crash.

"Kaylani!" he screams, the sound amplified by the sound of glass shattering.

"Shit!"

Without a second thought, I drop my own box and move toward the alley, instincts kicking in as adrenaline surges through my veins. The easy banter from moments ago is forgotten and all I can think about is finding Kay. I round the corner slamming into Creed's back and stumble, confusion mixing with fear as I peer over his shoulder.

What I see before us steals the breath from my lungs.

CHAPTER 22

Kaylani

I HEAD TOWARD THE back exit, my excitement building with each step. I pause just outside the door to Hux's office, hesitating at the sight before me. Hux is hunched over his desk, his face etched with stress. Papers are strewn across the surface, a chaotic mess that mirrors his apparent frustration. He mutters to himself, his jaw clenched tight, clearly consumed by the tasks at hand, likely related to the re-opening of The Omega Den.

A pang of guilt twists in my chest. Maybe I should give him a bit more time. He's been so dedicated, and I don't want to add to his stress.

I let out a guilty, silent sigh and step away from the door. The anticipation of seeing my nest still buzzes within me, but I can't shake the feeling that Hux needs a little more time to finish up. I'll wait a bit longer and let him wrap up whatever he's doing before dragging him away from his work.

I push open the back door with a smile on my face and scan the empty parking lot for Creed's truck. When it doesn't come into view, a sharp pang of anxiety and disappointment jolts through me.

Where are they?

Determined to find my pack, I round the corner, hoping they might have parked in the front to unload the liquor. My eyes stay fixed on the ground, trying to steady my nerves as I make my way down the short alley toward the front entrance.

Then, I catch the scent—cloves and tobacco, overpowering and suffocating. It hits me like a punch, making me freeze. The smell is so intense it feels like it's seeping into my very core. My body tenses instinctively, and an unsettling coil of recognition winds tightly in my stomach.

I've been imagining this scent everywhere for months, an unshakable shadow of my past. Every time I turned around, it was as if he was just out of sight, a haunting presence that drove me to the edge of madness. My heart pounds as I slowly raise my gaze, and there he is—standing in the alley, just as vivid as the nightmares that have plagued me.

Adam.

The sight of him sends a shiver of disbelief through me. I've been picturing him everywhere, convinced he was a figment of my mind's cruel game. All this time it made me feel crazy. But now, seeing him here, so real, so close, it feels like a punch to the gut.

For a moment, everything freezes. The world narrows to just him and me. I'm paralyzed, the image of him so clear and so present, it's as if time itself has bent to torment me. The intense ache of fear mingles with a twisted sense of relief.

I'm not crazy—he's here.

But the reality of it is overwhelming. My breath comes in shallow bursts, and I struggle to process the sight of him. I clench my fists, the knife digging into my side, grounding me with its dark promise.

It's time I get my revenge.

I know I have to move, to act, but the shock of seeing him after so many months of tormenting visions makes my mind reel. With my heart racing and the scent of cloves and tobacco burning in my lungs, I force myself to take a step forward, my eyes never leaving Adam's.

This ends now.

I narrow my eyes into slits, heat simmering just beneath the surface as all the horrors Adam has put me through rush back with brutal clarity. But instead of letting it ice my veins with fear, I allow it to seep into my bones like fuel to the fire. Until it's an all consuming, raging inferno.

His forced bite, the violence that left me broken—every cruel memory surges forward. The threat his family poses to those I care about. The fear and pain he has caused me. And now, here he is, intruding on my life again, demanding my attention.

Well now he will be the one to fear me.

"Why the hell are you here Adam?" I growl, my voice raw and seething with pent-up fury. I step tentatively toward the monster that haunts my nightmares, the hairs on the back of my neck standing on end. The urge to run, to flee from the dangerous alpha before me, is strong, but I crush it down.

No more running.

I won't be anyone's victim again. Today, I'm taking back my power. I inhale deeply, straighten my shoulders, lift my chin, and force my arms to hang loosely at my sides. Despite the appearance of calm, my heart pounds furiously.

Adam steps towards me, his movements deliberate as he comes to his full height. His eyes lock onto mine, a predatory gleam dancing in their depths.

"I missed you, little lamb," he purrs, his voice dripping with false sweetness.

I grit my teeth, the tension in my jaw almost unbearable. "I won't ask you again. Why are you here, Adam? We're over."

The darkness in his green eyes sends a shiver down my spine. The warmth and affection I once thought he harbored are long gone, replaced by a cold, calculating gaze. He's nothing more than a cruel alpha who sees me as a mere plaything, a tool for his gratification.

Fuck that.

I'll never let him make me feel that way again. This ends here.

"My mother says I need to break our bond," he continues, tilting his head to the side predatorily. His eyes roam up and down my body, a dark caress that feels like a thousand fire ants crawling across my skin. I swallow hard, feeling a surge of anger toward this alphahole. The only way to truly sever a bond with a feral alpha is through death. Words alone won't suffice; there will always be a lingering part of him in my heart, tainting it with his malevolence.

"Do you always do what Mother says?" I taunt, letting the bitterness show in my eyes. A sly grin tugs at my lips, defiant and unrepentant. I'm taunting him, urging him to lose control. I'm playing with fire and I'm ready to get burned. But if I go down, Adam is coming with me.

That is my dark promise.

Adam's nostrils flare at my taunt, his face darkening. I take another step toward him, pushing his buttons intentionally. My heart is restless, my hand itching to hold my knife.

"I thought you were the alpha of Pack Sterling, Adam? What happened? It seems you're still just a puppet on Mommy's strings. You have no backbone, letting an omega dictate every one of your moves." I let out a slow, mocking laugh. "You're nothing but a coward."

His eyes flash with fury, and his voice drops to a dangerous growl. "I am the Sterling Pack alpha. I rule this fucking city. My mother—"

I cut him off with another laugh, my voice cold and mocking, taunting him. "You're pathetic, Adam. Always hiding behind someone else's power. You've never been your own man. Always Mommy's little golden boy."

His face twists with rage, and he snarls, "You little bitch. I should have killed you when I had the chance."

His threat is empty, and I no longer fear him. If anything, I pity him. He will never have the bond, the pack, the strength I possess. And everything I'm about to do is for them.

"If that's how you feel..." I shrug nonchalantly, the casual gesture belying the storm inside me.

In a flash, he lunges at me, exactly as I anticipated. My hand dives into my holster, gripping the knife with steely resolve. I meet his charge head-on, the blade slicing through his gut with a sickening squelch. The force of his attack makes the knife sink to the hilt and his blood spills over my fingers, slick and warm.

I pull the knife free, the handle slippery with his blood, but I don't falter. I drive the knife into him again, and again, my eyes locked onto his, filled with fierce determination. Each stab is a release, a catharsis, a reclaiming of the strength he tried so hard to crush. It tanks my soul with darkness as his eyes widen in shock and he falls to one knee, his body slowly collapsing under the weight of my rage. The power it gives me is intoxicating.

"Kaylani please," he begs.

My smile is cruel. "Just remember, you asked for this. You wanted to break our bond. You tormented me. Used me. Never again will I cower to you adam. Ever," I sneer, echoing his own cruel words from so long ago.

He tries to raise a bloody hand, shaking and desperate, his fear fueling my fury.

"This is for Rebecca," I rasp, my voice trembling with the weight of my grief over losing my best friend.

I plunge the knife into him again, the blade slicing through flesh as if it's cutting through the very fabric of my pain. The release is bittersweet, a cruel comfort for the loss that still gnaws at me. His blood spills out, dark and pooling onto the ground beneath us, a grim testament to the justice I've sought for so long.

"For Hux," I say, my breath coming in sharp, ragged bursts. The knife meets his flesh once more, each thrust a release of the anguish I feel for the broken man who sacrificed so much for me.

I think of Hux's kindness, his protective strength, and the way he has stood by me despite everything. The stab is a tribute to his unwavering courage, to the way he's faced his own demons with quiet resolve.

To a true fucking alpha.

"For Creed. Your brother, Adam. For the fucked up shit your bloodline put him and Vaughn through," I continue, my voice cracking under the strain of my emotions.

The knife plunges in again, each stab echoing my fury and sorrow.

"And for me," I declare, plunging the knife into him, a raw release of all the fear, the hurt, and the powerlessness I've felt for so long.

I stab him again...

And again...

Each one driven by a desperate need to reclaim my strength, to turn my pain into power. This moment marks the end of his reign of terror.

His body convulses as my tears fall uncontrollably. I stand over him, shaking violently, my heart pounding with a chaotic mix of pain and liberation. The air is heavy with the scent of blood and the weight of my trauma.

Through my sobs and trembling hands, I feel an overwhelming clarity—a finality to the chaos that has plagued my life.

I continue to stab, my hands growing weaker with each thrust. The knife becomes slippery in my grip, but I keep going, driven by the need to erase every ounce of fear and suffering he inflicted on me. Until the tears stop flowing, until his green eyes stop haunting me.

As his life drains away, I watch the light dim from his eyes, feeling an unsettling calm despite the raging storm inside me. The scent of copper fills the air, and his blood soaks into my clothes, marking me with his final moments. The numbness should frighten me, but all I feel is profound relief.

Finally, I am free.

I can feel the bond between us dissolving, the fiery pain of his bite on my neck a brutal reminder of our severed connection. And that, even in death, he still causes me pain. I touch the bite mark on my shoulder, feeling the burn deep within me. A cry of anguish escapes me as I collapse to my knees painfully beside his lifeless body, his still warm blood soaking into my clothes. But no new tears fall. Through the agony, I manage a shuddering laugh, knowing Adam will never hurt me—or anyone I care about—again.

For the first time in my life, I feel a raw, transformative power. I throw my head back, gasping through the fire in my chest, embracing the warmth of my liberation.

They say taking a life changes you, and in this moment, I understand that truth more than ever.

I am changed, and I accept the darkness with a sense of twisted triumph.

CHAPTER 23
Creed

I'M SO TERRIFIED WHEN I see Kay sitting in blood that I can't seem to move. I'm rooted to the spot, my eyes locked onto the gruesome scene before me. At first, Adam's body doesn't even register—I'm blinded by the sight of my girl, drenched in crimson. My heart races, and my mind spirals into chaos as I imagine the worst, fearing she might be gone from me.

Finally, I look at Adam's lifeless body, and with a shaky hand, I pull off my hood. I can't tear my eyes away from my brother's crumpled form. I should feel guilt or remorse for his death, but all I care about is Kay—my tiny, my omega. Her head is bowed as she stares down at Adam's lifeless body.

"Kaylani?" Vaughn's voice trembles from behind me, his hand heavy on my shoulder. My omega instincts scream at me to comfort him, but I'm frozen. At Vaughn's voice, Kay slowly lifts her head. Her pink hair is matted with blood, and her stormy gray eyes meet Vaughn's vacantly.

"I did what you said."

My stomach coils with a mix of pride and anguish at the detachment in her voice.

Vaughn's breath hitches. "You did so good, doll. I'm so proud of you."

As Vaughn reaches her, Kay's beautiful eyes fill with tears that cascade down her face, mingling with the blood coating her skin. My omega instincts surge, and I drop to the floor in front of her, desperate to wipe away her tears. But they keep coming, relentless and heavy, and no matter how hard I try, I can't stop them. She screams, head tossed back, and it terrifies me. She sounds so small and vulnerable; all I want is to soothe the ache in her soul.

"You're safe, tiny," I say, pulling her against my chest. She turns her face into me, crying harder, her hands clutching my hoodie. Vaughn continues to murmur sweet words of praise in her ear, gently smoothing her blood-soaked hair from her face. After a few moments, Kay's tears subside, and she goes limp in my arms.

We may have ignited a war with my family for killing my mother's prized alpha, but I can't find it in myself to care right now. That's a problem for tomorrow. Today, my girl stood up for herself and defended herself. All I can think about is that she's finally free to be mine. Be ours.

I glance up at Vaughn, his dark gaze piercing mine with an intensity that's both dark and twisted.

"You're free now, Kay. Free to bond, free to love. Free of Adam," I murmur, reminding her that now she isn't bonded to Adam. She's free to choose who she wants. I just hope that still includes me.

Kay smiles softly, her lower lip trembling. She lifts a bloody hand toward me, inviting me closer. I let out a breath I didn't realize I'd been holding and take her small fingers in mine.

"Let's get you cleaned up," I say, turning to Vaughn. "I'm going to run her a bath. Get Hux and tell him what's happened. Maybe call Ghost? We need a cleanup crew."

He nods. "I'm on it. I'll meet you upstairs."

"Don't leave me!" Kay says sharply, looking up at Vaughn as he smooths her hair back gently.

"I'll see you in a minute, doll. Rest now, sweetheart."

"Don't worry, tiny. I won't let you go. I'll never let you go. Your pack is here for you. Always."

***

Carrying her into the bathroom, I set Kay down on the toilet seat and crouch in front of her. She curls into herself, her eyes fixed vacantly on her blood-stained hands. My heart aches as I reach out, pushing her hair away from her face, but she doesn't even register my touch.

You're safe with me, tiny," I whisper, my voice cracking with raw emotion. Seeing her so broken terrifies me, and I need her to come back to herself. I growl softly, cradling her face in my hands and forcing her chin up so our eyes meet.

"Look at me," I demand, my heart pounding so loudly I barely hear Vaughn and Hux approaching. I catch the scent of bitter chocolate, spicy sandalwood, and my caramel note—our pack's scent, mingling like a freshly brewed cup of coffee and everything my little omega loves. I inhale deeply, trying to ground myself so that I can reach Kay.

"Kaylani," I growl, shaking her gently. "You'll feel better if we wash the blood off. I won't leave you this time. I can't, okay?" My voice cracks, recalling the last time I saw this vacant look in her eyes, after Adam had tried to hurt her and Candi had forced Vaughn and me out of the bathroom. "Please, tiny, for me. Say something. Anything, baby. You're scaring me."

We're inches apart, so when her mouth parts slightly a rush of breath brushes over my face. I stroke my thumb across her cheek, but the haunted look in her gray eyes, filled with such raw pain, steals the breath from my lungs. Vaughn turns on the tap, filling the tub with Kay's favorite lavender body wash.

"Kitten, talk to us," Hux barks. Normally, I might have lost it at him for commanding her, but right now, it's what she needs. "Say something, Kay. Please," he says, softening his alpha command with desperation.

"He... He's dead," she stammers, her voice barely a whisper. My teeth clench in frustration and sorrow. She shouldn't have faced this alone. My eyes dart away from her face as my brother's lifeless body plays on an endless loop in my vision. The sight will haunt me, but right now, all I care about is making sure Kay knows she's safe and loved.

"I can't believe I killed him...that makes me... a murderer."

I look back at Kay, my heart aching at her words. "I can't say I'm sorry about it, tiny," I murmur, stroking her cheek again to ground myself. "What does that make me?"

My eyes search hers for answers, and a fresh wave of tears spill from her stormy eyes. Vaughn steps up next to me, placing a comforting hand on my shoulder.

"Let us take care of you now, doll," he says softly, gently pulling her to her feet and beginning to help her remove her clothes, his movements tender but efficient. He undresses her slowly, his eyes never leaving hers, ensuring she feels safe and cared for. He quickly strips down and lifts her into his arms, settling them both into the tub. I kneel beside the basin, ready to support her in any way I can.

He turns her back to him and begins to wash the blood from her hair with careful, loving movements. I reach for her loofah, squeezing a generous dollop of her lavender body wash onto it. I dip the loofah into the water, creating a frothy lather, and start to clean her face. Kay closes her eyes, letting her head rest back on Vaughn's chest. She looks peaceful, serene in that moment, like the doll Vaughn always says she is.

I move the loofah gently over Kay's shoulders, working to wash away the blood that stains her delicate skin. As I move it down to her breasts and stomach, my grip tightens, trying to be tender and careful despite the storm of emotions roiling inside me. My heart pounds with a mix of sorrow and relief, knowing she's safe, but that she's still grappling with the weight of what's happened.

"Kitten," Hux says softly, falling to his knees beside me. His dress shirt is rolled up to his elbows, revealing his muscular tattooed forearms, and he begins to help clean her, his touch gentle and deliberate. "The bond bite is healing," he continues, his voice soothing yet laden with an undertone of hope. "But the pain... it could be eased if you wanted. We can replace the bond, seal it properly this time, if that's what you need. It's your choice, though—unlike Adam, I would never take that choice from you."

Kay's eyes, once vacant, begin to soften with a hint of something more intense, more primal. She looks at Hux, then at me and Vaughn, her gaze shifting as she contemplates his words.

"If it's all of us," she murmurs, her voice trembling but filled with a new-found resolve. "I want to be bonded with all of you. Vaughn, Creed, all of us together."

A flicker of desire and longing ignites in her stormy eyes, blending with the pain that still lingers. Hux nods, his expression a mix of relief and affection. "We'll make it right, Kay. Together."

Vaughn, still holding her close, looks at me with a silent understanding. We know what needs to be done to help our omega heal and feel truly ours. As we prepare to seal our bond, we know our connection with Kay will be strengthened, giving her a promise of unity and safety amidst this chaos.

Vaughn and I silently communicate with each other, the lust in his eyes pulling a groan from my lips. Kay's eyes lazily open and land on me, her mouth parted. Releasing the loofah, my hands begin to caress her smooth skin, splashing the water slightly. Vaughn, too, begins to let his hands roam over her curves. Kay moans again, her legs falling open, and I dare to move farther down the planes of her body, my fingers dipping into her curls.

"You're so beautiful," Vaughn murmurs against the side of her neck. She arches her back, revealing her hard-as-diamond nipples, covered in bubbles. She tilts her slender neck to the side to give him better access. I dip my fingers into her folds and find her swollen clit, flicking my fingers over it and watching her face pinch adorably.

"Watching you blush has always been a favorite pastime of mine," I admit in a dark voice, thick with lust. "But this?" I dip into her pussy, flicking that spot deep inside her. "This, tiny, is way better." I growl.

Vaughn's hands come out from the water, running his thumbs over her nipples. His fingers pinch them firmly, pulling her pleasure higher as I flick her clit with my thumb in time with his movements. I'm practically panting. I'm leaning so far into the tub, my shirt is soaked, but I don't care.

I need to see her come.

Judging by the look on his face, Vaughn must feel the same as I do. "That's it, doll," he encourages her, before looking up at our alpha. "Kiss her. Swallow her moans."

I increase my pace on her clit, her body arching off Vaughn's chest.

"Isn't he hitting the spot just right, doll? Are you going to come all over Creed's fingers like a good girl?" he growls, nipping at her ear as Hux bites her lower lip.

"Yes," Kay moans into his mouth.

My cock is so hard it's pressing against my jeans. The bite of pain is uncomfortable, but I don't care. I'm desperate to see her come undone on my fingers. I clench my jaw and work her harder.

"Don't you dare stop, pet," Vaughn tells me.

Her body shivers deliciously. I watch the trail of bubbles travel down her breasts, leaving a sheen behind. I briefly pull my fingers out of her dripping pussy, and she moans in protest. But I quickly push them back in, adding another so that she's stretched exquisitely. She groans, her head falling back further, tangled in pleasure, with three fingers deep inside her and my thumb roughly making circles on her clit. I drive her closer to the edge, her breaths panting and ragged.

"That's it, doll. Come on, and then we'll go to your nest and fuck you properly," Vaughn croons.

He brushes her hair from her face, kissing along her jaw softly. Hux's hands travel to her nipples, plucking and rolling the hardened buds between his fingers. The water splashes up and over the side of the tub, all over the bathroom floor, soaking through my jeans.

She cries out as her pleasure peaks, her pussy gripping me so tightly I'm afraid I might come in my jeans like a pubescent boy—and she hasn't even touched me yet.

"Fuck," I say through gritted teeth as she comes down from her high.

I pull my fingers from her cunt, and she lets out a soft moan—the sweetest sound I've ever heard. I get up, reaching into the cabinet to grab a towel as Vaughn takes her in his arms and stands, a river of water falling off them both. Hux growls softly as he gazes at Kay, and I can feel the alpha instincts thick in the room. I pass him a towel and watch as he wraps her up in his arms, murmuring softly into her ear. His purring vibrates through the bathroom.

"Let's get you dried off and to your nest," Hux murmurs, his voice tender and full of care.

"My nest?" she asks. Eyes half-closed in the afterglow of her release, but still heavy with the weight of what she's been through.

My mind is a chaotic swirl of emotions, a mix of lust, guilt, and an over-whelming need to ensure Kay feels safe and loved. To make our pack whole.

As Hux carries Kay to her nest, Vaughn and I follow closely behind. The room is dimly lit, a soft glow from the bedside lamp casting a warm, inviting light. The nest we've prepared for Kay is a sanctuary of plush cushions, blankets, and the familiar scents of our pack, designed to offer comfort and healing.

"Everything is ready for you, kitten," Hux says softly as he gently sets her down on the nest. His voice is filled with affection, a promise of the safety and warmth we've worked to create for her.

Kay's eyes, still heavy with exhaustion and a hint of apprehension, soften as she surveys the nest. A sigh of relief escapes her, and she whispers, "I love it. It's perfect."

Vaughn and I settle on either side of her, our presence a comforting em-brace. Hux kneels beside Kay, brushing her hair back from her face with tender care. "You honor me by becoming mine, kitten," he murmurs, his voice thick with emotion. "I will protect you and our pack with everything I am. You will never be alone, and you will always have a place—a home, a family."

Kay's gaze shifts between us, her eyes reflecting a mixture of love and vulnerability. There's a soft trust in her expression that tugs at my heart.

Vaughn, sitting close, runs his fingers gently over her skin, his touch a soothing balm as we prepare to form our bond.

"I will always protect you, doll. You know that, don't you?" Vaughn's voice is deep and earnest, filled with a promise of unwavering commitment.

"Yes," Kay replies, her voice trembling slightly. "I know that, Vaughn. I'm free because of you."

Vaughn takes her face in his hands, his eyes full of pride and tenderness. "No, Kaylani. You are free because you're a fighter. You fought tooth and nail for your freedom, and I'm so proud of you."

Her breath hitches as Vaughn kisses her softly, the kiss a blend of passion and reassurance. My heart pounds in my chest, each beat echoing with a thousand unspoken feelings. I'm overwhelmed by the depth of my love for her, and for our pack.

I move closer, my touch gentle as I caress her cheek, my voice a low, reverent growl. "Tiny," I murmur, searching her eyes. You're the glue that binds our pack together. You've brought us all closer, made us a true family. Without you, none of us would be whole. We're stronger and more complete because of you. This bond we're sealing—it's not just about the past or the pain we've faced. It's about the future we're building together. You're the heart of our pack, and we're here to show you just how much you mean to us."

The air in the room grows thick with anticipation and a deep, shared desire. The bond we're about to form is more than just a physical connection; it's a pledge of our commitment to each other, a promise that we'll face whatever comes our way together. As the Pack Huxley.

CHAPTER 24

Hux

AFTER THE AFTERNOON SHE'D had we let her fall asleep, but impatience gnawed at me, a primal need simmering just beneath the surface. I needed to feel my omega come undone, to see the sweet surrender in her eyes. Slowly, I roused her from sleep, my fingers caressing her cheek softly, coaxing her back to consciousness.

She stirs, her lashes fluttering as her gaze meets mine, hazy with sleep but quickly sharpening with desire. She looks beautiful, laid out like a feast before me, her body a tantalizing display of soft curves and bare skin. I circle around to the end of the bed, her eyes never leaving mine, locked onto me with an unspoken plea.

"What is it you want, kitten?" I purr, my voice thick with hunger.

Her breath hitches, forcing her breasts higher, the dark pink tips hardening into diamonds. Everything about her is perfect—her scent, her warmth, the way her body responds to mine. My own body hums with anticipation, my alpha instincts roaring to life. The need to claim, to mark, to make her mine is overwhelming my senses.

Vaughn appears at the head of the bed, his presence grounding, yet somehow also igniting the tension further. I meet his dark gaze, a silent understanding passing between us. "Did you get what I asked for?" I ask, my voice low, almost a growl.

He nods, holding up the small box, the contents within promising pleasure and submission. Kay leans back to glance at Vaughn, her curiosity getting the better of her, but I quickly draw her focus back. I tisk in disapproval, a sharp sound that snaps her attention to me. "Kitten," I taunt, a slow smirk spreading across my lips. "Eyes on me, darling."

She quickly zeroes in on me, her tongue darting out to wet her lips, making them glisten in the low light. It sends a rush of heat through me, the sight of her eager obedience fueling my desire.

"Good girl," I praise her, my voice dripping with satisfaction, just to see how she will react. Her thighs suddenly press together, her body reacting instinctively to my words, and the air thickens with the heady scent of her rose pheromones. It wraps around us, intoxicating and sweet, a silent invitation that I am more than ready to accept.

"Damn, doll, you like it when our alpha praises you?" Vaughn's deep voice is gravelly.

Kay nods, her eyes flicking to his briefly before settling back on me. My cock hardens painfully. She's trying so hard to listen to me, and the power is going to become addictive if she's not careful.

"Where is Creed?" she whispers, like she's worried about speaking.

I raise a brow at Vaughn, who threads his hand into her pink hair, tilting her head back to make her look up at him. "He's watching you from behind the glass. He was being a bad boy and wouldn't let you sleep, so until he learns some manners, he doesn't get to touch you. Only watch you come undone from your alpha's and beta's tongues, fingers, and cocks."

She shivers, a low and guttural moan slipping past her lips at the dark promises hanging in the air. I chuckle, the sound deep and rough, loving the way her body responds to us, craving us just as much as we crave her.

"Now, kitten," I begin, taking the small box from Vaughn's hand and opening it with deliberate slowness. "If you want all of your packs cocks deep inside that pussy and ass of yours then you need to be prepared for it."

I walk to the top of the bed, positioning myself on the opposite side of Vaughn. Our omega is caught between us, her wide eyes tracking our every move.

"You just sit back and let our beta stretch your sweet ass and play with your pussy while I feed you my cock," I continue, pulling the plug from the box. The golden handle catches the light, the pink cat tail dangling from it a teasing promise of what's to come. I smirk, loving the idea of my kitten having a little pink tail poking out of her pert little ass.

"Do you want this, Kaylani? To be my little kitten? Let me play with you," I purr, my words dripping with dark seduction.

Her eyes flicker between me and Vaughn, uncertainty shadowing her gaze before she finally looks up at me with those mesmerizing gray eyes. The way she trembles beneath our gaze, the way her breath hitches as her need battles her hesitation—it all fuels the fire inside me.

"What about Creed? I need him too," she murmurs, her voice a blend of vulnerability and raw desire.

"Don't worry, kitten," I murmur, threading my fingers through her vibrant hair, savoring the silky texture. "You'll get all three of us before the night is over. But for now... I want to fuck that mouth of yours."

"Yesss," she whispers, her voice barely a breath. A wicked smile spreads across my face as I begin to remove my cufflinks, setting them carefully on the bedside table. The anticipation in the room thickens with every second. I pass the butt plug to Vaughn, watching as his eyes darken, his breath quickening with the same urgency I feel.

I strip off my shirt, the fabric sliding away to reveal the tension coiled beneath my skin. This is the first time Vaughn and I have shared, and while I thought jealousy might rear its head, it doesn't. Instead, the idea of my kitten being completely wrecked by us before I claim her officially turns me on more than I ever imagined.

"FUCK," she breathes, the word barely audible, as Vaughn begins to press the plug into her tight ring of muscles. Kay cries out, burying her face in the blankets as the intensity of the sensation washes over her.

"Arch your back, doll," Vaughn commands, his voice a low rumble of dominance that sends a shiver through her. She obeys instantly, her body arching as her knees press firmly into the mattress. Her hands dig into the blankets, soft pants filling the room, each breath an invitation, a plea for more. It's the perfect display of submission and need.

"Kitten, look at me," I demand, my voice cutting through the haze of lust clouding her mind. Slowly, she complies, her eyes locking onto mine, and Vaughn pauses, the head of the plug just barely inside her ass—a promise of what's coming.

"Once this tail is hanging from your perfect ass and my cock is buried deep in this sinful throat," I murmur, running my fingertips lightly across her neck, feeling her pulse quicken under my touch, "Creed will join us." My words leave no room for doubt, and I see a flicker of excitement ignite in her eyes as she slowly nods, her submission and need undeniable.

"Okay," she agrees.

I nod at Vaughn, and he pushes the plug firmly into place as he murmurs praise to our girl. Her body sags slightly, her entire body flushed a rose pink that matches everything in this room.

"Roll over, doll," Vaughn growls, delivering a firm slap to her ass. She obeys, her cry of surprise and pleasure sending a jolt straight to my cock. Precum leaks from the tip as I watch him spread her cheeks, revealing her glistening sex, her wetness coating her thighs. The sight of that pink little tail peeking out between her thighs only makes her more irresistible.

She lays back, her eyes wide as she looks up at me, her chest rising and falling rapidly, making her perfectly perky breasts bounce with each breath. I pull her closer to the edge of the bed, forcing her to tilt her head back slightly, exposing that slender throat to me. Vaughn and I both groan at the sight, the sheer beauty of her submission making the need to claim her all the more urgent.

Her pretty pink lips part at my command, and I watch with rapt attention as I smear my precum on her lips, marking her with my scent. Her tongue snakes out, licking my arousal from her lips, brushing against the tip of my cock ever so briefly. The sensation makes me hiss, a sharp sound of pleasure escaping me. Without hesitation, I shove my cock into her mouth, pushing until I hit the back of her throat. I hold myself there, feeling her body tense as she adjusts.

"Relax and take it all, kitten," I instruct, my voice firm yet coaxing.

Slowly, her throat relaxes, and I push further, testing her limits, seeing just how much of me she can take. Her hands land on my thighs, nails digging in as she struggles to maintain control. But she isn't pushing me away, instead she's pulling me closer.

FUCK.

Behind her, Vaughn settles between her thighs, his large hands spreading her legs wide before dipping his fingers into her slick pussy. Her body tenses again, reflexively trying to pull away, but I tighten my grip. Her moan of pleasure vibrates around my cock, sending a jolt of ecstasy straight through me. I groan, letting my head fall back as I begin to slowly pump my hips, each thrust forcing her to take more of me.

"Hollow your cheeks, kitten," I command, loving the way she obeys without hesitation.

"Such a good fucking girl, doll." Vaughn praises her as her slick sounds fill the air. The sound of Vaughn's fingers working her pussy fills the room, a symphony of slick, wet noises that only fuel my desire.

"That's it, kitten," I praise, my voice thick with need.

I reach down, plucking at her nipple, twisting it harshly between my fingers. She responds with a sharp intake of breath, her nails digging deeper into my thighs. The sight of her between us, submitting so perfectly, drives me wild.

"You look so beautiful between us, such a good girl taking my cock down your throat," I murmur, my voice a low rumble of approval, the tension building as Vaughn and I work in perfect sync to bring our kitten to the brink.

I pull out of her mouth, letting just the tip of my cock rest between her lips, giving her a moment to breathe. But Vaughn is relentless, his mouth working her harder, driving her closer to release. Her body shakes, trembling with the force of the pleasure building inside her, her back arching off the mattress.

Suddenly, Creed walks into the room, his eyes darkening as he takes in the scene before him. He stops in his tracks, his gaze locking onto Vaughn between her thighs.

"*Fuck me*, tiny. You look so damn sexy between our alpha and beta," Creed says, his voice thick with lust as his fingers trail along her trembling skin.

Vaughn increases his efforts, bringing her body to the brink. Her entire form coils, muscles tightening as she reaches the edge, and then she's coming so damn hard. I shove my cock back down her throat, making her gag on me, her cries of pleasure smothered by the thickness of my shaft.

I shiver. *Delicious*. Everything about my kitten is fucking delicious. Perfect.

"FUCK," Vaughn murmurs, his voice rough as he wipes his mouth with the back of his hand. He looks up the length of her body, his eyes locking onto Creed's with a shared understanding of what's coming.

I pull free of her lips, not wanting to finish inside her mouth just yet. Kay moans in protest, her disappointment palpable, but I merely chuckle, the sound dark and full of promise.

"Now, here's what's going to happen, kitten," I say, my voice low and commanding. "I'm going to remove that little tail of yours and replace it with Creed's cock."

Creed moves to help her sit up, his large hands gentle as he brushes her tangled hair from her face. She gazes up at me with eyes darkened by lust, her lips parted in anticipation.

"Then?" she prompts, her voice trembling with eagerness.

"Bend over, kitten," I demand, ignoring her question as my alpha instincts take over completely. "Spread your ass so I can remove my plug."

Kay obeys, moving to her hands and knees, her back arching as she presents herself to me. The sight of her dripping pussy and the small, pink cat tail swaying from her ass sends a jolt of raw, primal desire through me. My cock throbs painfully, aching for release.

"Damn, tiny, you're so fucking wet. I'm already jealous I haven't tasted you yet," Creed murmurs, his green eyes flickering to mine with an unspoken question.

"Alpha?" he asks, his voice rough with need. The fact that he's seeking permission to taste our omega stirs a desire in me I hadn't anticipated.

"You can taste her once she's fully satisfied and dripping with our cum," I growl, my voice thick with possessiveness. Kay moans, her body quivering as she looks up at me, her face a mix of longing and lust.

"Now get up there, omega, and make yourself useful. I've changed my mind, we need to stretch her ass further. She needs to be ready to take both of you, so leave the plug in," I command, my voice brooking no argument.

Creed chuckles darkly, his laughter a low rumble as he climbs onto the bed behind her. He moves deliberately, savoring each moment as he wraps his hand around the base of the pink tail and gently pumps it in and out of her ass. Kay buries her face in the pillow, a muffled moan escaping her as Creed inserts two fingers alongside the plug.

"That's it, tiny," Creed encourages, slipping his fingers free before he positions himself at her entrance. His hand settles on her back, holding her steady as he begins to ease past her tight rings of muscle. "Fuck, so damn tight," he groans, his voice thick with pleasure.

"Damn. Have you ever seen something so fucking sexy?" Vaughn growls under his breath, his eyes fixed on the sight of Creed filling her slowly. The way the pink tail settles between Creed and Kay is intensely erotic—a vivid contrast against her flushed skin. She does look incredibly sexy, the tail accentuating the curve of her ass.

Creed pauses halfway, giving her a moment to adjust, his breathing heavy as he fights to maintain control. The room is thick with the scent of sex and pheromones, the atmosphere charged with the primal energy of the pack.

"More," she demands, and I shiver with delight.

Creed sinks deeper into her, and a twisted satisfaction coils in my chest. This is just the beginning—Kay is about to experience what it truly means to belong to us, body and soul.

CHAPTER 25

Hux

As soon as her body relaxes, Creed picks up the pace, his head falling back in pleasure as he begins to pump in and out of her with a steady rhythm. I reach forward, plucking the tail between my fingers and giving it a sharp tug, making both of my omegas hum in pleasure.

Vaughn runs his hand up Creed's back, fingers tangling in his hair and yanking him back, exposing his neck. "I can't wait to see my mark on you again, love. But first, taste our omega's slick on my lips," Vaughn growls, his voice a mix of anticipation and dominance.

The two of them begin to kiss, Vaughn's hand gripping the front of Creed's throat, the intimacy of their shared moment intensifying the scene.

"Kitten," I say, drawing her attention back to me. Creed pulls back from Vaughn, his gaze meeting mine as well. "Creed is going to sit, and you'll keep him and my little kitten tail deep inside that sexy ass. I need to see my beautiful pussy before I knot you and make you *mine*."

Her breath hitches at the possessive tone, but she obeys, leaning her back against Creed's chest as he settles against the headboard, his cock still buried deep inside her ass. Both of them moan as the angle changes, the sensation clearly enhancing their pleasure.

"Such good little omegas," I croon, settling myself between their tangled legs. Kay's thighs fall on either side of mine as she adjusts her position, pressing her heat against my throbbing cock. Her slick folds drag up and down my shaft in a rhythm that makes me shiver with pleasure, each movement eliciting a satisfied moan from Creed over her shoulder. His hands grip her hips firmly as he relaxes against the headboard, his eyes closed in bliss.

I glance down at where our bodies begin to join, her slick arousal coating me as she sinks down slowly, inch by delicious inch. The sensation of her heat enveloping me fully makes both of us groan in unison.

"Just like before, doll. But this time, you'll have all three of us filling you up."

Kay moans as we shift forward, making room for my big as fuck beta. Vaughn slides behind her, his hands deftly removing the tail from her ass and tossing it onto the bedside table. He positions himself alongside Creed, pushing her forward until her cheek rests against my chest, the heat of her breath warming my skin. I pet her gently, smoothing her hair back from her face.

"That's it, kitten. Take all of your pack into this tight little body. You were made for us, baby girl."

Vaughn slides his massive frame between her and Creed, effectively shielding Creed from view. The absurdity of the situation is almost comical, but the pheromones filling the air are so intoxicating that laughter is the furthest thing from my mind.

"Are you ready, doll?" Vaughn growls into her ear, nuzzling her lobe.

"Yes, please. Do it," she hisses, her voice filled with desperate need.

"As you wish."

He eases in alongside Creed, sliding into her tight ass. A collective groan fills the room as all of us are finally rooted inside our omega for the first time. For a moment, no one moves, overwhelmed by the combination of sensations. I can feel both of them within her as Vaughn starts at a leisurely pace. He is the one in control of our pleasure and I'm okay with that.

I growl, my hands finding Kay's hips blindly. "FUUUCK..." I groan, my voice strained with the intensity of the pleasure.

Each thrust adds to the overwhelming sensation, amplifying our collective need. "How does it feel to be so stuffed with cock, tiny?"

Even though I can't see Creed behind Vaughn's massive shoulders, I can sense the raw desire in his voice, matching my own.

"Perfect," she whispers, her breath hot and teasing against my chest. Her body quivers and spasms around us as Vaughn thrusts deeper, his movements deliberate and slow, eliciting loud moans from her.

"Such a good girl, taking all of our cocks, doll," Vaughn praises, his voice thick with need and satisfaction. He grips her hips firmly, pulling her back onto him, and making her body arch even further while her pussy moves up and down on my cock.

My knot starts to swell, and I struggle to hold it back. The anticipation is driving me wild. "The thought of my knot holding all of my cum deep inside you is driving me insane," I growl, my voice barely controlled. "Seeing you swell with my pup…"

Her eyes flutter open, glazed with lust and unfulfilled desire. "You ready for my knot, kitten?" I murmur, my hand gently caressing her cheek and brushing her hair back. She nods, her lips parted as she pants through her pleasure.

She gasps, her body quivering at my promise. The idea of being filled and bred by us heightens her arousal. The anticipation of the knot and the thought of becoming ours completely makes her moan, eager for the fulfillment that's just out of reach.

"Say it out loud," Vaughn commands, his grip on her hips tightening, anchoring her between us. His authority makes her shiver with excitement.

"Want your knot, alpha," she admits breathlessly.

Vaughn's dark eyes lock with mine over her head as my knot begins to swell inside her. The pack groans in unison as her ass tightens around us, accommodating my knot. Kay whimpers, sweat making our bodies stick together.

"Take our alpha's knot. You're doing such a good job, my little dolly," Vaughn urges, his voice filled with raw need.

Finally, my knot locks us in place, and my release floods her pussy. I moan, my eyes falling shut as euphoria takes over. Vaughn's thrusts become more deliberate, each one sending ripples of pleasure through her body. "Relax, Kaylani. Be a good fucking girl and milk all of our cocks."

Kaylani's breathless whimpers fill the room, her body caught between the overwhelming sensations of being filled by all three of us. "No, kitten, you will look at your alpha as you cum," I growl, a mix of authority and affection in my voice. My hands grip her throat gently, guiding her chin up to force her stormy eyes to meet mine. The edge of ecstasy is almost within reach.

Creed's hands find her hips blindly as he groans through his release. "You were made for this, tiny," he whispers, his voice low and possessive. "To be claimed and filled by your pack. FUUUUCK."

Her moans deepen, her body tightening around us, her primal cries spurring us on. The sight of her—vulnerable yet strong—drives us all to see her completely undone. I thrust up into her as Vaughn slams her body down.

"You're perfect," I repeat, my hands trailing down her back, feeling the tension and release with each thrust. "Such a good girl."

Her eyes meet mine, showing the trust and submission we've forged through love and desire.

"You like that, doll?" Vaughn says darkly, his head tossed back as he roars through his release.

"Say it out loud," Creed demands, his hands gripping her thighs, holding her steady.

"I love it," she gasps, her voice strained with pleasure. "I love being your good girl."

The admission sends a thrill through me. I lean down to capture her lips in a fierce kiss, pouring all my affection and need into it. Kaylani's cries of pleasure grow louder, her body arching and straining as she is overwhelmed by the sensations. The room is filled with the sounds of our passion, a primal symphony of our bond.

"Now that you're mine, kitten, it's time for our pack to finally become one." I smile at her, my mark on her neck bringing me a joy I never thought I would have.

Slowly, I pull her by the hips, letting Vaughn and Creed slide free. With my knot still firmly in place, I drag us up the bed and get comfortable, Making her sigh in contentment.

"Are you ready to make us whole, Kaylani? To be the piece that binds us all together?"

She nods, looking at each of us in turn. "I've never wanted anything more," she admits softly, and my heart swells with pride.

"Good. But I think our beta and omega need to solidify their bond again first, don't you think?" I search her eyes, letting her know she gets to decide how this goes.

"Yes," she replies.

We turn to Vaughn and Creed, who are lost in each other's arms. Vaughn breaks their kiss, resting his forehead against Creed's.

"You said you forgave me, pet. But do you trust me?" Vaughn asks softly.

Creed's breath hitches. "Yes, love. I trust you."

"Thank fuck," Vaughn murmurs, kissing him once more before trailing kisses down Creed's neck to the same spot where I had just marked Kay, biting him softly. Creed groans in pleasure and returns the gesture on Vaughn's shoulder, bonding them together as one again after so long apart.

They turn to us, both breathless, and I can feel the love they have for each other in the air. I know it's time to bond us together officially. Kaylani sniffles watching them, her happy tears pooling on my chest.

"I'm so happy to finally see you both accept each other again," she chokes on the words.

Creed takes her hand in his and kisses her palm gently. "I love you, Kay. So fucking much. You are the reason we were able to come back to each other, you know that, don't you?"

Vaughn nods in agreement. "You're ours, doll. Ours to protect, ours to love. If you'll have us."

Her breath hitches as she nods into my shoulder, rubbing against the fresh bite I have from her.

"Of course I want you both," she says softly.

Our pack moves closer, one on either side of the bed as both brush their lips against each of her shoulder blades. Their eyes meet mine, waiting for my permission.

"Claim her," I growl. "Show our omega just how much you love her."

At the same time they seal their bond with Kaylani, I grab Creed's wrist and bite the sensitive flesh there. My heart aches with the bond between us immediately.

I lick the small drops of blood before grabbing Vaughn's wrist to do the same. "You're my beta, Vaughn, and you're worthy of this pack. Of being a member of Pack Huxley, now and forever. Do you accept?"

The room shudders as I wait for him to respond. Once I bite him, our bond will be complete—whole, finally—but he needs to choose this, because he already rescinded Creed's bond once. Once I bite him, there'll be no going back this time.

"Claim me, alpha. Seal us all together, please," he growls, his dark brows pinched together as his wrist comes to my lips.

I growl and bite down. A rush of emotions swirls inside me. I'm not sure if they are mine alone or the combined pack now sealed together. But it's the most intense feeling I've ever felt, and it feels so right, so perfect, that I know we are stronger together.

"I love you all so much," Kay whispers.

"Mine," I purr, nuzzling her neck, feeling the warmth of our bond enveloping us. "Now, rest, my omega. You've earned it."

Vaughn and Creed pile back into Kay's nest, all of us together... It feels right. Like we have always been a pack. I gaze at Kaylani, my omega, sandwiched between my pack, and I can feel the primal satisfaction swelling within me. The sight of her, flushed and glistening, her needs satisfied, sends a rush of dominance and protectiveness coursing through me.

This is where she belongs. In our arms. Her pack. Her protectors. Her home.

As she drifts off to sleep in our arms, I look at Vaughn and Creed, my heart swelling with pride and contentment. This is our pack, our family, bound together by love and loyalty. And I know that nothing will ever come between us ever again.

Epilogue

Kaylani

DRIVING TO EDEN'S HOUSE for Sunday dinner, the weather is chilly and I pull my thin sweater tighter around my shoulders, wishing I would have just come in jeans and not this dress. My pack surrounds me, their scents combining into a sweet coffee aroma that settles over me.

Creed, in the backseat beside me, his hand warm on my knee, gives me a reassuring smile. I glance over at Vaughn in the passenger seat, his large frame barely fitting, and he turns slightly, his deep, steady presence calming my nerves. Hux, focused on driving, offers a gentle smile in the rearview mirror.

I feel a surge of happiness looking at each of them, knowing they're here for me. But beneath that joy, there's a current of sadness and nervousness. Bex should be here. She would have loved them, loved seeing me happy. Her loss still ebbs and flows through me, and the thought of introducing my pack to my family without her feels like a knife twisting in my heart.

As we get closer to Eden's, the familiar sight of the neighborhood brings a flood of memories. Sunday dinners were a staple growing up, a constant in a world that often felt uncertain. The thought of stepping back into that world, even with my pack by my side, makes my stomach twist with anxiety. I just hope my family can see how much these men mean to me and how they've helped me find my way back to myself.

I take a deep breath, trying to steady myself. We've been through so much together, and tonight is just another step in our journey. My pack's presence is a balm to my nerves, and I know, no matter what happens, we'll face it together.

"You doing okay, tiny?" Creed asks, his hand sliding over the backseat and resting on my bare knee.

I nod, and give him a half-smile as his thumb draws lazy circles on the inside of my knee. His touch, gentle and reassuring, sends warmth through me, soothing the anxiety that's been gnawing at my insides.

"Are you sure? You seem like something is bothering you. You know you can talk to me about anything, right?" Creed's brows furrow with worry.

I blow out a breath. "I haven't been to a Sunday dinner at Eden's for over a year. It was a staple growing up. We had so many people coming and going on Sundays. I swear, Eden was trying to feed the entire neighborhood," I say, a fond smile playing on my lips.

Creed grins, squeezing my knee. "Eden sounds amazing and I can't wait to meet her officially, and the rest of your family, tiny."

I nod, glancing out the window but not really seeing much of the world go by as I try to get my emotions under control. I remember the last time I came, I had brought Bex with me.

"I miss her so fucking much," I whisper.

Some days, I'll laugh at the memories of my best friend, other times I cry at the void she left behind. Today her absence feels like a fresh wound that won't stop bleeding.

"She would be so proud of you, Kay," Creed says softly.

My eyes shoot up to his, my lips wobbling into a watery smile. "How do you know?" I murmur.

Vaughn, sitting in the passenger seat, turns slightly to face me. "Because you've become everything she believed you could be," he says, his deep voice steady and reassuring. His hand reaches back, resting on my shoulder with a firm, comforting grip. Vaughn's touch, like Creed's, is filled with unspoken promises and unwavering support.

Hux, behind the wheel, chimes in without taking his eyes off the road. "We've all seen it, Kay. You're strong, resilient, and you've brought us together as a pack. She would be proud of the woman you've become."

I feel a warmth spread through my chest at their words, the love and support of my pack enveloping me. I look around at each of them, feeling incredibly grateful. How did I get so lucky to have these amazing men in my life? Each of them has played a part in my journey, helping me heal and grow. I don't know where I'd be without them.

As we sit at a stoplight, Creed turns his body to face me more. "You defended yourself when you had to. You fought for the pack you wanted." He tucks my hair behind my ear. "How could she not be proud of you? I am."

His pale green eyes search mine. I'm not sure what he sees, but his shoulders visibly relax and a lazy smile graces his full lips. I have the urge to kiss him.

Sucking his bottom lip into my mouth, I feel the warmth of his breath mingling with mine. He responds instantly, his hand tightening on my knee as his other hand cups the back of my head, fingers threading through my hair. The kiss deepens, and for a moment, the world outside the truck fades away. It's just us, tangled in a web of emotions and unspoken words.

When we finally pull apart, we're both breathing heavily. Creed's eyes are darker now, filled with an intensity that sends a shiver down my spine. "Well I feel better," he admits, his voice rough.

"Me too," I chuckle, my fingers still resting against his cheek. The connection between us feels electric, alive with the depth of our bond.

He smiles, a genuine, heart-stopping smile that makes my heart flutter. "We're going to be okay, tiny," he says, his thumb brushing against my jaw. "No matter what happens, we're in this together as a pack."

I nod, feeling a sense of calm wash over me. "Together," I agree.

The light turns green, and Hux reluctantly pulls away, turning his attention back to the road. The rest of the drive is quiet, but it's a comfortable silence, filled with the unspoken understanding between us.

As we approach Eden's house, my nerves start to creep back in. The familiar sight of the large, welcoming home brings a flood of memories, both happy and sad. I take a deep breath, trying to steady myself.

Hux parks the truck and turns to me, his expression serious. "You ready?" he asks, his hand finding mine and giving it a reassuring squeeze. His grip is firm, grounding me in the moment.

"Ready as I'll ever be," I reply, squeezing back.

We get out of the truck, and as we walk up the path to the front door, I can already hear the sounds of laughter and chatter coming from inside. It's a comforting sound, one that makes the knot in my stomach loosen just a bit.

Eden opens the door before we even have a chance to knock, her face lighting up with a warm, welcoming smile. "Kay! It's so good to see you!" she exclaims, pulling me into a tight hug. She smells like cinnamon and home, and I feel a lump form in my throat.

"It's good to see you too, Eden," I manage to say, my voice thick with emotion.

She pulls back and looks me over, her eyes twinkling with mischief. "And who are these handsome men?" she asks, her gaze shifting to my pack.

"This is Hux, Vaughn, and Creed," I introduce them, and they each step forward, offering their hands.

"Nice to meet you, ma'am... officially," Hux says politely, his grip firm and steady.

Vaughn nods, his deep voice respectful. "Thank you for having us."

Creed smiles, his charm evident. "We've heard so much about you."

Eden waves away their formality and pulls each of them into a hug. "None of that 'ma'am' business. Just Eden is fine," she insists, laughing.

As we step inside, People are bustling around, setting the table, preparing food, and chatting animatedly. It's chaotic in the best possible way.

"Come on, let's get you all something to eat," Eden says, leading us toward the kitchen.

As we navigate through the crowd, I spot familiar faces, each one bringing back a flood of memories. My sister and her pack, Shade and Liam, are off in the corner chatting.

It's overwhelming, but in a good way.

I feel Hux's hand on the small of my back, grounding me. Vaughn stays close, his protective nature soothing, while Creed's playful presence keeps my spirits high.

We finally make it to the kitchen, where Eden hands us plates heaped with food. "Eat up, there's plenty more where that came from," she says with a wink.

We find a spot at the large dining table, and as we sit down, I can't help but feel a sense of belonging. This is my family, my home, and for the first time in a long time, I feel like I'm exactly where I need to be.

Creed leans over and kisses my temple. "It's nice to see where you come from, tiny. Eden must be proud," he murmurs.

I smile, feeling a warmth spread through my chest. "It's good to be back," I whisper back, and for the first time in a long time, I truly believe it.

Hux sits next to me, his hand finding mine under the table. His touch is steady, reassuring. "You've done an amazing job, Kay. Bringing us all together, finding your place. We're proud of you."

Vaughn nods, his deep voice filled with sincerity. "We wouldn't be here without you. You've made us stronger, better."

Creed's eyes sparkle with mischief and affection. "And a lot happier," he adds, making me laugh.

Later, as the evening winds down, I find myself sitting outside on the porch, the cool night air refreshing. Hux joins me, his presence a comforting anchor. "You okay?" he asks, his voice gentle.

I nod, leaning into him. "Yeah, just needed a moment to take it all in. It's been a lot."

He wraps an arm around me, pulling me close. "You're doing great, kitten. We're all here for you."

Vaughn and Creed soon join us, and we sit together in companionable silence, the stars twinkling above us. It's a perfect moment, one that I'll cherish forever.

"We're a pack," I say softly, my heart full.

Creed nods, his smile warm. "Always."

Vaughn squeezes my hand, his grip reassuring. "Forever."

Hux kisses my forehead, his love a steady presence. "Together."

As I sit here, surrounded by the love and support of my pack, I know that we can face anything. Bex's memory lingers, a gentle reminder of the journey that brought us here. And while her loss still aches, I find solace in the fact that she would be proud of the woman I've become, and the family I've found.

At this moment, on the porch of my childhood home, I realize that I'm not just home – I'm finally whole.

THE END

Stay tuned for Candi's story and what happens next between the Hounds and MC.

Knot So
SWEET
LEATHER & LACE
PART 1

MISS RENAE

Prologue

Ghost

THERE'S A WAR BREWING in Sterling City, a storm that's been building for far too long. The Hounds have crossed a line this time, a line that should've never been crossed. The Steel Serpent MC couldn't let it go unchecked, not when the stakes were this high.

Abducting omegas, bringing Heat into our city—it was despicable, even for a stray. Titus's hunger for power had led him to align with Michelle Sterling's twisted vision, using a heat stimulant to control and conquer every unmated omega. It had to be stopped, by any means necessary.

The casualties our city has suffered over the last six months alone are unforgivable. The memory of those lives lost twisted my stomach with a seething rage that I could barely contain. The air was thick with anticipation, gnawing at the edges of my nerves and refusing to let go. But tonight, we would ignite the first flame. Tonight, we would make our move.

Enough was enough.

Miss Renae

I AM A WHY-CHOOSE PNR and Omegaverse author—a dog trainer by day and a spicy romance author by night. I lost a part of myself when I became a mom. Post Partum Depression and PTSD affect my daily life to this day. As an avid reader, books are my escapism, but I kept DNFing. So I decided to write my own on October 22, 2022. I found that part of myself again in my own stories. Writing is my therapy, and I hope you love my stories as much as I do! Follow your dreams; I am. Thank you for taking a chance on me! Be sure to follow me to get all updates on upcoming releases!

Tiktok> @missrenaeauthor

Facebook Group> Miss Renae's Pack of Freaks

Instagram> @missrenaeautho

My older books

Blood Moon Bonds Trilogy

The Gemini Duet

Dark Legion MC: Hellfire

Fated: A Club Euphoria Novella

Made in the USA
Coppell, TX
21 November 2024

40704342R00142